The Tide
Aurora

By Brandon M. Bryson

Preface

On Wednesday, May 26, 2010, I was working as the Executive Director for a large assisted living community. I had been working there for one month shy of two years and I enjoyed it very much. I loved the people I worked with, and I loved the people who we cared for. I looked forward to many years in that industry, experiencing the joy that comes from the work of caring for others.

Early in the morning that day, the owner of the company stopped by to visit. This was not unusual, as he lived in town, and he usually came by about once a month. He followed up on some business items, and then gave me the biggest shock of my life... He fired me. I had never been fired in my life, and I thought things were going quite well in the community. I spent the next couple of days saying my goodbyes and wondering what I was going to do next, as I embarked on one of the most difficult things I've ever faced, unemployment.

I spent the next several months looking for work in the same industry, which I had come to love. I was not having much luck. The job market was heavily saturated with very qualified individuals, all applying for the same few jobs that opened up. I renewed my insurance licenses and gave that a try, but it did not work out for me, as the expected 80 hours a week kept me from my family too much and the sales program I was taught to use was not in line with my ethical standards.

It was during this time that I had a dream. It was not a dream like most others; vague, confusing, and hard to remember details. It was a dream that actually had a storyline; it was exciting, adventurous, and heartwarming. I woke up, so thrilled about this amazing dream, I immediately started writing it down. It was about 2 o'clock in the morning and I was writing everything I could remember about what I had just dreamed. Then I went back to sleep, slept the rest of the night, and woke up, determined to turn what I had just dreamt into a great story I could share with all who would let me.

A couple months went by, I had some good interviews in the healthcare industry, but nothing ever came of them. In November 2010, I decided that I needed to go to my plan B and I started looking for work in transportation. I renewed my commercial drivers license and was actively looking for a job driving a truck, hopefully local, as I did not want to negatively affect my family values.

A few weeks later, I got a job driving a truck for a local company, with a route that allowed me to be home most every day. I was grateful for that. Over the next several months, I worked on my story when time permitted, I took voice notes while driving and developed it into what you are about to read. I hope you enjoy my story as much as I do.

Chapter 1 - The Dream

It was a calm night at sea for the crew of the ship they called Danielle. It had been a great day of fishing and at sunrise, they would head home, having caught their weekly maximum haul in only two days.

Although the waters were peaceful, the dreams of Greg Landers were nothing but calm. He tossed and turned in his bed, as if he were struggling from some unseen force, trying to drown him in the depths of the sea. He vividly envisioned it over and over again; the storm of all storms. In his dream, he and his crew had been fishing all week with very little to show for it. They were tired and angry, their tempers flaring at even the slightest annoyance. Friends were at each other's throats like old west gunfighters, who always wanted nothing short of a battle to the death. It was on the night before heading home virtually empty-handed that the storm came. It started slowly, with only some typical rain showers. Greg was stationed at the radio, listening casually to the weather service for any storm or hurricane warnings; there were none. Suddenly he was startled by a thunderous crack as the skies moaned a warning to the entire crew of impending danger.

Instinctively, Greg yelled, "Every man to his emergency station! Prepare for a CAT5 storm! Secure all lines! Bring in all nets! Life vests on everyone! I mean everyone!" The men knew Greg well enough to know that he did not overreact. They responded immediately. Every man raced to his station and braced himself for the severe wind and monstrous waves expected in a category 5 storm. They were an experienced crew, but experience wasn't enough to help them this time. Waves crashed down angrily on the Danielle, a 40 meter long fishing boat, tossing it around like a toy in a little kids bathtub. Water pelted their faces and rendered their vision useless. They were manning the ship on instinct now.

As worried as Greg was about the condition of his ship and safety of his crew, he remained at the helm, and held onto the wheel with all his strength. His hands were clenched white, his veins bulging from his forearms, he was determined to steer that ship out of the storm, the greatest storm he had ever encountered. He feared for his life, but more so feared for the lives of his crew and their families who waited for them each time they were out at sea. They trusted Greg and looked to him as a father figure. He loved them all like family. Pushing those thoughts away, Greg focused on his task and tightened his grip.

The waves continue to descend, tearing the ship apart, piece by piece. The bow received the first major blow, knocking out Greg's primary navigational points. Then the stern was blasted with an enormous wave, followed by an ear-splitting crack that Greg immediately knew meant he had just lost his rudder since the wheel in his hands lost all tension. Greg cried out to God. He was beginning to lose hope. Was his entire crew doomed to death at sea? Just managing to hang on, beginning to resign himself to his watery fate, Greg closed his eyes and prayed, one last time, for a miracle. At the moment he finished his prayer, the ship began to cut through the water, like a warm knife through butter. Greg couldn't comprehend what was happening. There was no explanation for the change in direction. The ship was not reacting to Greg's efforts to steer. He realized his effort was in vain, the ship no longer needed him. The crewmen were confused just looking to each other for an explanation. Greg stopped yelling orders. He frankly didn't know what to tell his crew. The ship was guiding itself! Finally he called out, "All men maintain your positions! You all know how easy it is to be surprised by a storm." The men stayed in their places, and frankly could not do much else. Most of them were frozen with fear and confusion. They were in a state of utter disorientation, and had no clue what was guiding their ship.

The ship continued its mysterious course. Every turn was precisely correct. Greg stopped checking his usual navigational instruments and took a step back from his steering wheel position. It was obvious to him that the ship was being guided by some external force, but he had no fathomable explanation for it. He thought there might be a malfunction of his steering hydraulic systems, but why was every turn perfect? The ship was acting like it had a high-tech, advanced steering system, which would sense errors in the ship's steering mechanisms and make automated corrections, but Greg's ship was not that advanced. Still confused, Greg began to relax, and his heart rate began to slow as the waves subsided and the ship continued her smooth course.

Seconds later, Greg's heart rate spiked with alarm as he heard the sound he dreaded most … a scream, followed by splash. It was the sound of one of his crew going overboard, a captain's worst nightmare. But this time his fatherly instincts bristled, and his subconscious recognized that the terrified scream was not of a man, not of one of his crew, but rather it was a voice of a little girl, his precious daughter, Kara. His recurring dream had just turned into a nightmare of the worst kind. Worse, somehow, than the pain he would imagine of having to tell a family that he lost their father at sea. In his dream, he suddenly realized that his five-year-old daughter had been swallowed by the sea.

It was right at that moment that Greg awakened, as he always does, to find the splash he had heard in his dream was real. He gathered his senses and realized he was awake, drenched in a cold sweat, resting in his cabin on his boat. He could hear the familiar sounds of the sea water lapping up at the ship, and he knew there was no real danger. He subconsciously reminded himself that the splash he had heard was just Kara, jumping into the water to swim.

This dream had repeated itself almost nightly for several years. His crew told him he should seek professional help, but he never would. Although he hated the dream and very much hated waking up with the horror so often, there was something about this dream that he cherished, and he did not want any doctor, or psychologist to take that away from him with some high-priced therapy or drug regimen.

His little Kara jumped in the water, first thing in the morning on every calm day at sea, provided that Greg had given her permission to do so the night before. He got to his feet, and quickly went down to the bow where he knew he would see her blond head bobbing up and down, swimming, like a fish, grinning from ear to ear. She loved swimming in the water as much as Greg loved fishing at sea. She would swim at every chance she had. She was a fantastic swimmer, even though she had never had a single lesson. Her dad told her it was because she was born of the sea. She liked it when he told her that, it made her feel warm inside. Greg called out to her, "Good morning, beautiful!"

"Good morning, Daddy. Did you sleep well?" Kara asked innocently. Greg had never told her about his nightmare. He saw no reason to; he would never want his little girl to have any reason to worry about her Dad. It was absolutely essential to him that he give her a strong sense of safety and stability in every aspect of her life.

"Yes, I did. Thanks for asking. I will see you in a few minutes at breakfast." Greg went back to his cabin to change and clean up for the day. As he did, he pondered in his heart how grateful he was to have a fantastic, beautiful little daughter, a good ship and crew, and good health. He had been raised to be grateful for the good in his life and this was definitely one of those mornings, when it was easy to recognize his blessings.

Chapter 2 - Becoming a Fisherman

Greg Landers loves the sea. Being the son of a fisherman, his childhood memories involved being schooled by his mother, Helen, while his father, Robert, and his crew fished, mostly one week at a time. He learned all the necessary things other children learned in traditional school, with the added benefit of individual attention, and a lot of field trips to the ocean. He spent summer months with his grandmother in a small town inland about 30 miles. His friends there loved hearing the stories he would tell about his father and life on the fishing boat, like the time they came across an abandoned shipwreck. He told them about how he and his father explored the old ruins, just like pirates, and found old coins, rusted out swords, guns, and maps, a lot of maps. Greg was wondering if those maps would lead him to hidden treasure someday. Greg's father let him keep some of his favorite maps and a few coins to show the other boys when he was staying with his grandma. He never did show anyone the maps, but enjoyed sharing the coins with his friends. Everything else was kept in a storage shed as a shrine to all their adventures. Greg and his friends loved and idolized his father.

Greg loved to watch his dad fish. His eyes would visibly get brighter, an uncontrollable smile would stretch across his face, and he would become calm, just like a perfect day at sea. Greg loved fishing as much as his dad. As a young boy he told people that he could hear the sea calling to him, almost like it was singing songs to him. People would warn him of the legends of sirens, but he always thought that was silly talk.

Greg had white-blond hair when he was young, which slowly became darker as he got older. Now in his late thirties, his hair was a rich brown on top and streaked with gray near his temples. He was built like an iron-forged male physique statue from the lifetime of working on fishing boats. His mom always told him that if he ate fish for most of his meals, he would be healthy and live a long life. So far that was proving true; he was a perfect picture of health and fitness. He was not a tall man at just under five feet, eleven inches, but because of his muscular stature, he appeared taller; most people described him as intimidating. Even though he was not middle-aged yet, his skin was starting to look very leather-like. Thick skinned, literally and figuratively, is how some described him. This just added to his tough appearance. He was often told that he looked like he could be an action movie star.

His parents had a small home in a coastal town of Fulton, located in the bay area, just northeast of Corpus Christi, Texas. Robert and Helen Landers met there in the South Texas area, where Robert was born and raised. Robert's commercial fishing business was profitable and provided means for Helen to raise their children close to the water. Although Robert was at sea most days of the week, Helen knew he was never far away. Their home was along the beach of Capano Bay, so in the evenings, when she was especially missing him, she would walk down to the beach and wade in the water. She could feel his touch as the cool water crossed her feet and legs.

As a child, Greg would sometimes ask his mother, "Mommy, why do you walk in the water so much?"

She would always answer with the truth, "Greg, when I am in the water, I can feel your fathers touch. I know that we are both in the water together, even though the miles separate us."

When Greg heard his mom talk like that, it helped him love the water too; he spent many hours each day, playing in the water. He loved to bring his toy boats to the beach and pretend he was the captain, giving orders to his crew, like he imagined his father doing out at sea.

When Greg graduated from high school, his parents encouraged him to attend college in San Antonio. Greg told them over and over that he wanted to be a fisherman, but each time they argued that fishing was a hard life and they wanted him to go to school and have the opportunity to choose whatever vocation he wanted.

"Fishing is what I want!" Greg insisted, "Mom, Dad, there's something out there for me. I love the sea. I love the way I feel when I'm out on the boat. I know I've never told you this, but," he hesitated, looking down, and clasping his hands together, "there is something more."
Greg was sitting with his parents at the kitchen table after dinner. He felt that the time had come to make a final decision about the direction of his future. It was of utmost importance to him to help them understand how he was feeling.

"What is it Greg?" his mother asked lovingly, sliding her chair toward his, and reaching her hand out to his hand, "what more is there that you need to tell us."

"The sea calls to me," Greg said, "I hear it when I'm laying down at night. I hear it when I am studying my schoolwork. I hear it when I pray. I hear it the most when I am in the water or on the boat."

"When you pray," asked Helen? "We have always taught you to listen to your heart and listen to God's voice when you need direction. Is that what you mean?"

"No, it's not the voice of God," said Greg, with a reverent tone. He believed in God. He believed that God answered prayers, and gave guidance to all his believers who asked in faith, but this was not what he was trying to tell his parents.

"It's something else," he began to explain. "I hear what sounds and feels like a woman's voice, calling to me from the sea. Sometimes I hear it in the wind, and I turn around to see who's there, only to find I am alone." His parents were focused on his every word. They could feel in their hearts that their son was telling the truth." I told you I hear it when I pray. Well, sometimes it is so clear, so loud, it has startled me. I've felt God's spirit at church, and at my baptism, and I have heard his voice of direction when I have prayed for answers, just like you taught me, but this is different. I know this is not the voice of God."

"What is the voice saying?" asked Robert, sincerely hoping for an answer he could somehow relate to, or explain.

"I don't know," Greg said hesitantly. "Please don't think I'm being childish or crazy." Greg really wanted to explain what he was feeling, but the words were so hard to find. "I don't know what the voice is saying because it's as if the voice does not speak in our language. I can feel it and I understand that it is for me. I think it's a message, calling me to the sea." Greg was sure his parents would now try to talk him out of this "imaginary" voice he was hearing, but they didn't. They just looked at him with all the love a parent could have. So he continued, "There is more. The voice is not really talking. It sounds more like a song, like someone is singing to me because they are hoping I will understand the song."

Robert's demeanor abruptly changed. His brow furrowed as he thought of what he has always believed, for most of his life, to be folklore, or myths about the sea. *"Should I tell my son what I am thinking?"* He thought.

Seeing his dad's expression, Greg asked, "What, dad? You think I'm crazy, don't you? Do you think I am just a boy afraid of going off to college, trying to come up with some reason not to? Is that right?"

"No Greg, it's not that at all." his father responded respectfully. "it's just that... well, I will just go ahead and tell you what I am thinking. It will likely come out sounding like I have lost my marbles, but please know that I am just sharing with you things I have heard all my life."

"Now Bob," Helen interjected," don't go telling us one of your old seamans tales, you know how I feel about that; I have asked you not to fill our kids' minds with all those nonsensical stories."

"I know, honey, I know." Robert continued. "but I feel it is time for our Greg to hear something about this, at least one of the old stories that relates to what he is currently feeling or experiencing."

As Greg was watching and listening to his parents talk, he got the feeling they both knew something that he did not,"Uh, hello; what in the world are you talking about dad?"

Robert looked back at Helen and she smiled, giving him non-verbal permission to continue, "You see, son, there are stories that the old seamen would tell about songs sung to men through the ages, while they are out on the sea. They always say these songs are calling to them, drawing them to the sea, like the lover they have waited for their whole life, it makes them feel that if they could just find the source of the song, all their dreams would finally be realized. They spend, sometimes, all their lives, looking for the source of these voices. Some of them go mad, trying to figure it out, some of them sail deep into the ocean, without resources to sustain their voyage, and are never heard from again. Some of them actually dive deep into the waters, so deep that their gear they take with them cannot withstand the pressures of the sea, and they end up dead, crushed by the depths of the ocean waters. Then there are some, who just mysteriously disappear." Robert stopped at that point.

"Now I have your attention, don't I, my boy?" Robert said, seeing that Greg's eyes had widened, and curiosity, like a cat, had covered his face. "You see why this legend makes such a great story? You can surely also see the wisdom of your mother in insisting I do not tell these old tales to you and your brother, especially as you were growing up."

"Yeah, dad, I understand. It is just a legend. Tell me more, please." Greg just had to know what his father wanted him to know about this old tale.

"The legend has it, that the voices the seamen would hear…" Robert paused, knowing that this might be where he would lose the attention of his son. Not to mention the sure laughing out loud he would get from his sweet wife. In fact, he couldn't recall if he had ever shared this much of the legend with her before.

"It's said, and really believed by some old time seamen, that the voices they would hear were mermaids." he then stopped, fully expecting to hear the laughter and expressive disbelief.

Greg just looked at him dumbfounded, like a kid who just learned the truth about Santa Claus.

"Mermaids?" Helen blurted out with a tone of sarcastic laugh, "Now you have gone too far Bob; how about we get out some pie for dessert and forget the rest of this nonsense?"

Robert continued," It is believed that these mermaids sing to fishermen in order to lure them far out to sea where they can take their lives as vengeance for all the fish they have disrespectfully captured and killed. It has even been said that the only way to ward off these voices is to encourage one of your crew to search for them until lost, as sort of a sacrifice. Your ship would then be safe from the temptations of the songs from then on."

"You mean sirens, dad? I've definitely heard stories about sirens."

"Yes, I believe that's what people call them nowadays, but remember they're mythical."

"Have you ever heard the voices Dad?" asked Greg, not knowing what his father was actually thinking at this point. Helen also leaned an ear in more intently, wanting to hear exactly how her husband would answer this question.

"No. No, I haven't son." his father responded emphatically. "I have never heard these voices and never will. I don't believe it is true. I don't believe there is anything to hear." As soon as these words escaped his mouth, he knew he had just offended his son.

"You don't believe me dad?" asked Greg. "How can you not believe me? Why would I make this up?"

"Greg, it's not that I don't believe you," Robert knew he had to be careful with his words, "I do believe you; I just don't believe the old legend about mermaids or sirens."

"Mermaids, ya right," laughed Greg. "Neither do I, dad. You were the one who brought it up." Now all three of them were laughing, and quite jovially too, as if to release some tension they had all been feeling as the conversation concluded.

The laughter soon faded into smiles; smiles of love and understanding from parents to their child. They all felt it and relished times like these when they felt like a close family, a family that could be together for all time.

Greg was the first to reopen the conversation. He was not finished talking about this. "So what do you think I am hearing then, dad?" he asked, sincerely, with respect to a wise father from a trusting son.

"I don't know Greg. I just don't know."

"Do you think I am imagining it?" Greg asked. It was important to him to know exactly how his father felt about this.

"Greg, my friend, my son," Robert spoke softly, " as I listened to you describe your feelings and experiences to your mother, I saw the look in your eyes as you did. I know you were telling the truth." Helen began to agree, but Robert looked at her and asked his wife kindly to let him finish his thoughts. "Son, as you were telling us about these experiences you have had, I could feel something inside me, telling me you were speaking truthfully. Similar to the way you explained, it was like the feeling of God's spirit, but very different also. I believe you, son. I do not know exactly what to tell you about the voice you say you hear, but I do believe you." He then looked at his 18-year-old son, who was as strong as he was, and tough as nails, now visibly teary-eyed before his parents.

Greg's mother saw this too, "What's the matter, honey?"

"I don't know what to do now," Greg said, "I know you want me to go to college because you believe it will be the best thing for me, at least, that is what you have said you think; but I am confused. I know the importance of education, I really do. I just feel I should be at sea. I feel like it is my destiny, my calling, if you will. I want dad to continue teaching me everything there is to know about his ship and crew and the ways of a Fisherman's life. I want to spend my life at sea." At this point, Greg was speaking very passionately. The tears continued, but they were tears of joy and conviction. It was obvious to his parents that he had given this some serious thought, and he had made up his mind that following in the path of his father, was what he wanted out of his life.

Robert jumped to his feet, grabbed his big son and squeezed him with a hug. Neither of them have ever felt it before; a hug that joined them, not as father and son, but as two men who just became one in spirit and direction. They both knew the next few years would be the toughest and the best they would spend together

Helen then joined in the embrace; all three were now crying, tears of joy, love, and dedication.

Later that evening, Robert went to Greg's room as they were preparing for bed. "Son, there is one more thing I want to tell you about."

"What's up Dad?"

"I want you to know, as an old fisherman, having spent my life on the sea, that I have seen some very strange and unexplainable things," Robert put his hand on Greg's back, "you have too."

"I have?"

"Yes, you have. You may not appreciate all the things you have seen at this point in your life, but someday you will." Robert stood up and walked to the bedroom window, "as a man of the sea, and because of the many unexplainable things I have seen, I have to make decisions for the boat and our crew based on facts, as well as occasionally fiction."

"What do you mean?"

"I said I do not believe the old legend I told you, but you should know that I still take precautions for my crew, just in case, the legends are true. You have to respect the sea and everything you know, and don't know about it."

Greg looked very puzzled.

"You see son, although I can't tell you I believe the crazy stories about mermaids and other mythical creatures, I still feel it is important, to respect the life of the sea, and all its inhabitants, just in case. That is why you will always see me taking great care, and choosing where we lower our nets, making sure we are not damaging any of the coral or bottom dwellings, which are in place as a natural habitat for sea life. You will notice that we are always careful to limit the amount of bycatch and other waste that we pull in with our nets. We do everything we can to treat the sea with respect." Robert looked his son right in the eyes and continued, "Greg, if you do the same, you will never have to worry about all those strange legends, true or not"

"Thank you Dad," Greg gave his dad a hug, "and thanks for being willing to teach me everything you know. I love you!"

"I love you too, son. Good night. We've got a big day on the water tomorrow!"

Chapter 3 - The Boat

The next five years seemed to fly by faster than time should move. Greg learned everything he could from his father about trawling. Trawling was the type of fishing they did, which was basically using a net to drag through the water to collect the fish. Robert's ship was considered small to midsize. It was about 20 meters long by 5 meters wide at mid and aft ship. It was powered by a single diesel engine, producing 250 horsepower. It pulled two nets at a time, in a fashion known as beam trawling. This is when two nets are used, one on each side of the boat, held out by a very sturdy beam and lowered into the water with warps, or a series of ropes. They would lower their nets mid-water, and their usual catch was flat bodied fish, such as the snapper and gulf flounder.

Robert named his boat after his wife Helen's favorite song, Edelweiss. Helen liked this song so much because she loved flowers. She had quite an impressive garden at their small home.

The Edelweiss was operated by Robert, Greg, and their crew of eight other men. Robert was, of course, the captain. They had a first mate, who assisted Robert, and acted as captain when he was off duty; a boatswain, who is in charge of the six hired deckhands. Greg acted as a deckhand, while he was out with his father, although he was, in all reality, training to be captain of the Edelweiss, or better yet, captain of his own ship.

Greg had been saving his money throughout his childhood, and now into his life as an adult, with one goal in mind; buying and operating his own fishing boat. Robert now knew this and supported him and his efforts, even paying him some of the profits of each weekly haul. Greg appreciated this and always told his father he would take care of him after he retires to pay him back.

Robert would respond, "Don't worry about it, Greg, you've earned what I am giving you. You are the hardest working deckhand I have ever had on the ship and you deserve to be rewarded for that. You stay with me long after all the other men have gone home after a haul, you have pretty much given up your social life to help me grow this business of ours to reach the successful levels we currently have. You know, son, I never thought I would see the day when my little boat would be as successful as it is, and I owe a lot of that to you and your insight, wisdom, and downright hard work. Not to mention, you are my son, and I love you!"

Another five years later, Greg came to his dad to say, "Dad, I think I have enough money to put toward a down payment to purchase my own boat."

"That's great, son! What size boat are you looking at?" Robert was very interested in what research Greg had done, knowing he always seemed to be properly prepared for big decisions.

"I am interested in getting something very much like yours, Dad, only newer" Greg hoped he was not offending his father, by wanting something better than he had, "not that I don't like the old lady Edelweiss, but I want to get something newer, something that will last me a lifetime if I need it to. You understand, right?" Greg had never really feared being straight with his Father, especially after working close together for the last 10 years. They had an extremely close relationship and were always honest with each other.

"Of course I understand, Greg" Robert had been waiting for this conversation for a long time. He really wanted to help his son realize his dreams. "Have you ever thought about getting something bigger? Perhaps a trawler that could pull four nets at a time, two lower-level and two mid-level?" Greg was listening intently to his father as Robert continued, "that would open up the world of lower swimming fish for you. People really love the Halibut, and they'll pay good money for it too."

"I know they would, but I am not interested in bottom trawling, it stirs up too much unintended sediment and damages too much natural sea life for what you get out of it. I would rather stay with mid-level trawling." Greg was proud to be able to show his father that he had actually done some research about this, and wasn't just trying to jump in, expecting success, just because his father had success. "However, since you brought up the idea of a bigger ship; that thought has crossed my mind." Greg paused and changed his tone lower and spoke slower, "Did you know that shrimp trawlers catch about 50% of the red snapper quantities that we, as red snapper boats, catch on an annual basis? And did you know that they usually just treat it as bycatch, discarding it as useless?" Greg and his father had had discussions about bycatch on several occasions. It was important to Greg that his ship was as responsible as possible with the delicate sea environment. Bycatch is the sea life that trawlers catch in their nets, which was not intended to be caught. It is then thrown back into the ocean, but most of the time it is dead by then. It would upset Robert and Greg, very much, to hear of some of the boats, when they had large mammals or turtles in their nets, who would not take every effort to care for those animals properly to ensure they get quickly returned to their environment. There have been times when they have actually had Dolphins in their nets. It was their practice to attend to the beautiful mammal as quickly as possible, even if it meant losing the rest of their intended haul. To their knowledge, they have never had a Dolphin on their boat long enough to cause it any lasting harm.

"I was not aware it was that much, Greg. I think I see where you might be going with this idea." Robert had talked to Greg about shrimp trawling at times, especially as the prices people were willing to pay to eat the little things kept increasing. He wanted to get into shrimping, but always felt like it was past his time, that it was too late in his career to start something new. He then let Greg continue.

"Dad, if I could get a bigger boat, one that I could drag four nets at once, I could get into the shrimp business and also continue our red snapper reputation." Greg was beaming with excitement, "I would be able to do this responsibly, too, greatly reducing the amount of bycatch I have to discard because I would keep the red snapper I catch with the shrimp haul! The cost of the boat is a concern, though. I will have to put in more time for that, perhaps another five years working for you, and I will have the funds to buy a boat big enough for shrimping. Do you think that would be best?"

Robert felt so much pride and satisfaction as a father at that moment. Standing before him was a grown man, the age of 28, his son, Greg. He was wise beyond his years, he was as hard a working man as he'd ever known, he was passionate about what he believed in, he respected God, and loved all men without bias; and now he could also see some of himself in the eyes of his son, with all the good he hoped he has installed in him shining through. He was so proud, he had to fight back the urge to grab his son, and just cry with joy, as they had done 10 years ago when they started this journey together. It's not that there would be anything wrong with embracing his son right now, it's simply that he had more business to take care of... Something else he wanted to talk to Greg about regarding his future as a commercial fishing boat owner.

"Greg," said Robert, "your mother and I have been talking about this day for several years now; the day that you would be ready to start your own business, with your own boat. We knew this day would come and we have been looking forward to it, as well as planning some way we can add to your success as you take this very important step in your life." Robert was so excited to present his plan that he could hardly gather his thoughts.

"What do you mean, Dad?"

"Your mother and I have spent more time apart during our 30 years of marriage than any couple should have to, as you well know, and we are both looking forward to my retirement. We are longing for when we can spend all our days and nights together, you know, doing what old folks do," he was saying with a smile and a wink.

Greg interrupted, "You're hardly old, Dad, you've got a lot of good years left in you."

"I know, I know. That is not what this is about, I feel young as ever. This is about spending time with the love of my life. Spending the time with her that I've always promised to do." Robert could see the confusion on Greg's face as to why he was talking about this right now.

"What are you trying to say, Dad?" Greg was indeed confused where the conversation was going, but asked, "Are you going to retire? 'Cause I don't know if I can do this whole captain thing without you, especially since my plans are to save until I can get a bigger boat."

"Let me just say yes... and no," Robert went on, expressing his thoughts to Greg, "try not to jump to conclusions, just hear me out on this one. Like I said, your mother and I have been planning this and I would like to see what you think of our idea."
"Okay Dad, let me in on what you've been planning." At this point Greg didn't know if he should be excited, disappointed, or bewildered. He was a little of each.

"I want you to be as successful as possible as you get your own boat and start your life as a captain and I'd like to think that if I were by your side during this process; you'd have the greatest chance of success," Robert elbowed his son in the ribs in gest, "but I can't always be there."

"I agree with that, Dad, but you aren't suggesting I take over the Edelweiss, are you? How would the crew feel about that?" Greg loved the crew and worked very well with them and he felt they reciprocated that feeling to him, but this type of a transition gave him cause for concern.

"No, Greg, that is not what I am suggesting." Greg took a deep breath as his Father continued, "I am going to sell the Edelweiss and use the money to help you get the size and style of boat you want for your future business."

"Are you serious!?" exclaimed Greg, "That is a lot of money, how would I repay you? I have to pay you back. I wouldn't feel right about it if I didn't have some way to repay you. You have already done more than I could imagine or expect to help me be successful, I can't let you do this without a repayment plan."

"You didn't let me finish," Robert said as he gave further explanation, "I would be investing in your business. Therefore, I would, like you've expressed, expect some kind of return for that investment. First, you would pay me the salary of a highly qualified, experienced first mate aboard your ship for the next year or so, until I officially retire."

Greg said, "I am okay with that, I could think of no better first mate to have, but there has to be more. Employing you as my first mate for a few years does not pay you back for your investment in my ship."

"Again, let me finish, my boy. This is my revised retirement plan I'm laying out for you. The next part is this; after I officially retire, your mother and I are paid 10% of all your net profits, until neither of us are living." Robert stopped to allow Greg to process his thoughts for a moment. "Does that sound fair to you? That way you have the best chance for success, and you can make due on your promise you have always made to take care of us in our old age." Robert stopped, having shared his idea, and not being one to elaborate with unnecessary details. "Feel free to take some time to think it over for a while."

"Think it over!?" Greg said, almost shouting, "What is there to think about? I could not come up with a better idea if I thought about it the rest of my life! You truly are the best father a guy could possibly have! Thank you dad. I love you."

"I love you too, son I love you too!"

"So what do we do next?" asked Greg, "Do you want me to help you get the Edelweiss ready for sale and listed on the Interweb, as you call it?" He laughed.

"That's a nice offer, Greg, but not necessary. That is one of the best parts of this plan. First mate Bruce wants to buy the Edelweiss." Robert was grinning from ear to ear, "We've already come to an agreement on price, and discussed with the crew who stays with him, and who comes with us."

"What the…? When did you…?" Greg was searching for the right way to ask his question, "How did all this get done without me being aware?"

"Greg, you are a hard worker. I respect you like crazy for that," Robert was chuckling as he talked, "but you need to take more breaks, give yourself a rest once in a while. While you were working your guts out, the rest of us had time to make some arrangements without your knowledge."

"Touché," said Greg, "nice move, Dad." He then grabbed his father for that embrace they'd both been holding back.

Chapter 4 - Danielle and the New Crew

It didn't take Greg long to find the ship he wanted. It was a late model, barely used trawler that was previously owned by a fisherman who couldn't make ends meet and ended up losing his business. It was the perfect size for what he had in mind, 40 meters in length and about 12 meters wide. It had twin diesel engines producing a total of 800 horsepower. It was already outfitted with nearly everything he would need to get his fishing business up and running immediately. It had all the nets, the beams, the generators, the pulley systems, the below deck coolers, a nicely equipped galley, enough berths and cabins to sleep a good sized crew comfortably, as well as great captain and first mate quarters. He couldn't believe how perfect this ship was and the asking price was in his range! They were asking $2,250,000.

"That's a lot of money," Greg said to the man in charge of selling the boat.

"This is one mighty vessel too," he responded with a typical salesmanship tone, "worth every penny of the asking price."

"Perhaps," Greg said, looking at his dad, who had come with him. "I don't see a name. What's the ship's name?"

"We removed the name out of respect to the prior owner, which was his only request. He felt strongly that the name had something to do with his failure." the salesperson replied.

Greg and Robert turned to each other, smiled, and Robert said, "I think you should make him an offer."

Greg had saved $300,000 over the last 10 years and Robert sold the edelweiss for $700,000. The sellers of the boat needed to get it off their books and agreed to Greg's offer of an even $2 million. With 50% down payment, an excellent first mate and an experienced crew, financing the other 50% came easily, even in a struggling economy, and in a tough industry.

The crew consisted of Greg, as captain, Robert as his first mate, a boatswain named Billy, a mechanic named CJ, the medic Brian, who was a licensed practical nurse, and seven other deckhands. The medic and mechanic both worked as deckhands as well. Brian and four of the deck hands, Jim, Wayne, Tina, and Brett, who also did the cooking, all came from the Edelweiss, and were reliable crewmen. Billy was recruited from a Norwegian ship; he was looking to move his family to the United States, and wanted some warmer weather, too. He was very experienced for his age, 30 years old, and spoke very good English, with a light Dutch accent. CJ was a recent graduate of a technical school in Corpus Christi, which he completed merely as a technicality, having worked on boats nearly his whole life. He had worked on fishing boats nearly every summer since he was 14 years old. He was now 30 years old, and completed schooling with the help of and under the advice of Robert, as a safety and regulation requirement, having worked with him many years. Since Greg's boat was new to him, it had to be licensed and registered under current guidelines, which required a certified mechanic and a licensed medic be part of the crew.

With the ship purchased, and the crew hired, it was now time to name the new boat. Greg didn't have anything in mind, although he had been thinking about it for years. Robert would not even offer suggestions.

Robert told his son, "The name of the boat reflects its true Captain. The name must come from you."

Greg talked to some of his crew about it, but they all felt the same way Robert did, the name should come from the captain. They were all true seamen; one of the seamen beliefs was that the ship, once named, became just one more member of the crew guided by the captain.

It was now the last weekend before they set sail on the first voyage, and Greg did not have a name for his ship. He didn't know what he was going to do. He believed, like the crew did, the ship takes character when, and only when, the captain gives her a name. "What is the name!?" he shouted to himself. "She's your ship! What are you going to name her!?" he was starting to get very frustrated with his lack of inspiration for a name. It wasn't that he couldn't think of any name, plenty were popping into his head, names, like Allison, Sydni, Rebecca, Kimberly, all the names of past girlfriends. That wasn't good enough for his ship. He needed a name that would stand the test of time.

Greg decided to turn to the Internet for help in finding a name, "There are thousands of names online," he thought. "What would the crew think of him if he came to the maiden voyage of the ship with no name?" He kept thinking to himself, "I need some help with this; I need some help finding a name," but he knew no good seaman would help him. He decided to turn to God for guidance. He found a quiet place and pleaded to his higher power, asking what he should name his ship.

It was a short time later, while looking through a list of names and their meanings that the name came to him. It jumped out of the computer like it was three dimensional; it leapt right off the screen and into his mind and heart, like it had always been there. DANIELLE, he read, DANIELLE. The name means judged by God. That was exactly the name he was looking for. That is how he had always tried to live his life, he cared more about how he was viewed by his higher power, with little regard for what others thought of him. He lived to be judged by God, not by man.

He sat there looking at the name on the screen. It felt good. It felt right. He pondered about the name Danielle and how to explain it to his crew when they, undoubtedly, would ask him. He decided to take a walk and think about it some more so he headed out along the water's edge.

He had only been walking a few minutes when he heard the voice he had not heard in several years, but just like in times past, he could not understand what it said. He stopped walking and turned to face the water. He heard the voice again and thought he could understand it this time. "Are you saying my name?" he spoke into the night air in a loud, but delicate voice, "Are you saying a name? Are you trying to tell me something? Who are you?"

"My name is Danielle," he heard clearly, as if carried to his ear by the wind.

He couldn't believe what he had just heard. Was it real? Was it the same voice he had heard so many times in his past, or was he imagining things due to the panic and stress he was experiencing leading up to his big day as captain of his own ship?

Then he heard it again, this time it also spoke peace to his heart and soul in a tangible way, "My name is Danielle."

He still did not know what the voice was. Surely it wasn't his ship speaking to him all those years, "That's insane," he thought to himself. What he did know, though, is that the voice was still real after all these years of being silent. He knew he had received some help, and he knew he had found his ship's name, the DANIELLE.

He rapidly went to the marina, where the ship was docked; having called a painter on the way, explaining that he would pay him triple time if he would help him get the name painted on the ship before Monday morning. He met the painter there, and he began immediately. It was then that Danielle began to come to life. She was beautiful!

Everyone on the crew, their families, local businessmen, and the city government who showed up for the christening ceremony and sendoff agreed that the name fit. "It has a ring to it." they would say. The wives of the crew all agreed that the name made the ship sound and feel safe and secure. Some said it was appropriate for a ship captained by Greg.

Greg loved the response the name Danielle was receiving.

Greg stood at the bow of his ship and shared some words adapted from the old Lord Richard Burton:

"For thousands of years, we have gone to sea. We have crafted vessels to carry us and we have called them by name. These ships will nurture and care for us through perilous seas, and so we affectionately call them "she"

"On this day, we raise our voices in thanks to God and celebrate the birth of a new family aboard the Danielle."

"To the sailors of old," Greg shouted, "and to the Danielle!"

"The moods of the sea are many and ever-changing, from tranquil to violent. We ask that this ship be given the strength to carry on. The keel is strong, and she keeps out the pressures of the sea."

"To the sea, to the sailors of old, to the sea!"

"Today we come to name this lady Danielle, and send her to sea to be cared for, and to care for our crew, her family. We ask God, the sailors of old, and the sea to accept Danielle as her name, to help her through her passages, and allow her to return with her family safely"

"To our God, to the sailors of old, to the sea, TO THE DANIELLE!!" [1]

With the christening and the naming complete, the crew said goodbye to their loved ones, boarded the Danielle, and headed out for their first trip.

The maiden voyage began without incident, and the Danielle successfully headed out for her first week at sea.

---

[1] 1 Commander Bob, Don't Forget the Christening, www.commanderbob.com

Chapter 5 - Sapphires and Emeralds

Kara Danielle Landers was not that different from any other little girl you might know or see; except that she had a couple very distinguishable, physical attributes: her hair and her eyes.

Kara's hair was as blonde as blonde can get; it was so blonde, that when in the sun, she would often have people tell her it looked white. They would tell her it looked like it was glowing. Her eyes were deep blue, like the ocean, not the typical blue that most blue-eyed people have; her eyes were more of a royal blue color, they had the appearance of a perfect sapphire. Rarely, would anyone look into her eyes without pausing and making a complementary comment about their "amazing and unique" color. There was something more, though, about her eyes....

Kara was in the backyard playing at dusk one evening as a child. Greg had to come out to let her know it was time to come inside for the evening. When he looked at her, she looked back, but neither of them said anything initially. Greg just stopped and stared into his daughter's blue eyes.

"What is a Daddy? " Kara innocently asked.

"Your eyes, Kara, there is something about your eyes."

"I know, Daddy. You have told me how much you like my eyes and how pretty they are like my mommies." Kara was smiling and almost singing. She loved the rare occasions when her Dad talked about her Mom and hoped he would now.

"Yes, I have," Greg just kept looking at her, "but there is something different tonight."

"What's wrong with my eyes tonight?"

"Nothing at all, honey, but they are not the deep blue that they normally are. Your eyes have changed color; they are more of a green color now. They look like emeralds. They normally look like sapphires."

"What's an emerald Daddy? "

Greg bent over and picked up his little girl, holding her in his arms, "an emerald is a rare stone, it is a very beautiful, dark green color. "

"My eyes are blue, not green."

"Yes they are; your eyes are the bluest I have ever seen, but tonight they look green, they are one of the most beautiful things I've ever seen. They remind me of a certain area of the sea that most people never see. It is very deep, very pure, very beautiful water. The water there is a deep green color, unlike anything I've ever seen. That's what your eyes look like tonight."

"Thank you, Daddy," she said as she squeezed his neck in a hug.

As the days, months, and years would pass, those closest to Kara would come to realize that her eyes were very different. They would change color in the evening light and into the night. Sometimes her grandpa would call her the "chameleon girl."

Kara has very fair skin, but is unusually fortunate to not sunburn very easily. Greg told his daughter how rare it was to have such fair skin, but not have to constantly apply sunscreen, especially with all the time she spends in the sun and swimming.

Greg tells his friends and new acquaintances, when talking about his daughter, about how unique she is. He is a very proud father. He tells them about the comments he always gets from people about how beautiful she is. She is his only daughter, and he had little experience with raising children, but he knew it was not normal for so many people to use words like beautiful, stunning, and exquisite to describe a young child. People did though, and he was very proud of that, but also tried to keep his pride for his daughter in check, knowing that a lot of people are sensitive to overly proud parents.

It was indeed true that Kara had unique physical characteristics, but it was Kara's personality, and not just her personality, but rather, her spirit, that was not like anyone else's you could ever meet or know. Greg would learn more about this the following day, which would be Kara's first time on a fishing trip with him and his crew.

"Kara, you need to get your pajamas on and get to bed," Greg spoke loudly toward the back of the house, where Kara's bedroom was, "tomorrow is a big day, and we have to get up very early and head down to the marina."

There was no response.

"Kara?" He hollered a little louder, "did you hear me? "

Still, there was no response, so he got up from his desk, where he had been preparing his logbooks for the week ahead, and walked back to Kara's bedroom. When he knocked and opened the door, he could see she was already in bed asleep.

"What an amazing little girl I have," he thought to himself as he turned, closed the door, turned off the hall light and walked back to his desk, "I am truly a blessed man."

Chapter 6 - First Time Out

The man Greg had contracted as his mechanic, Corby Jones (everyone called him CJ), was one of the roughest, meanest, and most crude men most people had ever met. Most people would describe him as the very definition of mean. When you looked at him, you were scared, very scared. He would never have been Greg's mechanic if Greg hadn't already known him through his father. CJ was Robert's mechanic for many years, long before his life became so filled with hate and anger.

"Why are you so angry all the time? "Greg one day asked, after having known CJ a while, and feeling comfortable enough to do so.

"Greg, life has dealt me an awful hand."

"An awful hand? What do you mean by that?" Greg was asking sincerely.

"I haven't always been this way. I used to be very happy, very pleasant to be around. I won the heart of a beautiful woman who blessed my life with two beautiful children. Life was good, I felt like the king of the world," CJ stopped.

"Then what happened?" Greg inquired, "I can see that there is a light in you, but it just seems to be hidden by something else."

CJ went on," let me be more honest with you… I like to tell people that life dealt me an awful hand, but that is not exactly the truth. The truth is that life has not "dealt me a bad hand," so to speak. I selected the cards I have through my own poor choices."

Greg listened intently, knowing CJ had something on his mind that he wanted to share.

"You see Greg, about eight years into my marriage, I started making some choices that were not good for me, or my family. I knew what I was doing was wrong, but I kept making those same bad choices over and over again, until I eventually lost everything. My wife divorced me and because of my actions, I had a criminal record, so the courts gave her full custody of our kids. She took them and moved far away. I don't even know my own daughters. It breaks my heart every damn day."

"Wow CJ, I'm sorry," Greg said as he reached his arm and put it on CJ's shoulder.

"I appreciate that, but don't be sorry man," CJ insisted, "I do not expect, or want, anyone to feel sorry for me. I made my choices and I'm living with the consequences. I know that I am usually not fun to be around, I hold a lot of anger inside me; however, you should know that I do not think poorly of those around me, my wife, or anyone else in my life now, or before. My anger is toward myself, toward my past, toward my mistakes."

Greg waited a moment before he made the comment, "CJ, thank you for sharing that with me, I appreciate it. May I share something with you?"

"Sure, whatcha got?" CJ answered.

Greg looked CJ in the eyes and said, "I know there is no reason for you to take advice from me, but here's some anyway... Don't hate yourself. We all make mistakes, man, some more than others, some worse than others, but we can all move on from them. You have already taken the first step; you know what your mistakes were and now you just need to stop punishing yourself and recognize that you no longer make those choices. Your life can be happy again, you just need to let it in."

"People have tried to tell me things like that before. I have thought about it and am unsure how you do it?" CJ spoke, very hesitantly, not wanting to intrude on his captain's personal affairs, so he said slowly and softly, "I mean, I know you have suffered terrible loss too, and you don't have to talk about it if you aren't feeling it. How do you maintain your happiness?"

"Our circumstances are very different, which I'm sure you realize, but I will just let you know that I made the choice. I realized my attitude was my choice," Greg removed his arm from CJ and stepped back in a reflective manner. "I knew that I needed to be someone positive for my little girl, so I made the decision to never let her see the pain I feel inside about losing her mom. I never, ever, want her to have any reason to think that I am not the happiest man in the world to have her as my daughter." Greg had a tear in his eye, "And truthfully, most days I feel like I am."

That was all CJ and Greg spoke to each other about that day, and had never spoken to each other again about the topic.

The day CJ met Kara started as an ordinary day on the Danielle while they were getting ready to go out to sea. He and the crew were aware that they would have a special guest this trip. So they were trying to be on their best behavior.

Kara was excited for her first time out with Greg, she was 5 years old now and he felt it was safe for her to go with him now that she would be able to walk around well and he knew enough to keep her safe under most circumstances; she was also very well behaved and good at following directions. She was also an extraordinary swimmer, better than most adults. Greg felt good about bringing her with him.

Up until this trip, when Greg would go out to sea, usually a week at a time, Kara would spend that time with her uncle Jeff, Greg's brother, and his wife, Courtney. They did not live very far away from Greg and they had no kids of their own and were happy for the opportunity to help Greg out and have Kara with them most weeks. It was almost like the three of them were a family of their own, and they loved, treated, and respected each other like they were.

CJ, with the rest of the crew, we're loading and securing the supplies they would need for the week out at sea. CJ was a large man and did much of the heavy lifting. He was in the process of lifting a large crate of bait into place when one of the handles came loose, and he dropped the nearly 100 pound crate on his foot and ankle. This happened right when Greg had Kara by the hand, walking in CJ's direction so they could be introduced. Greg and Kara came around the corner just in time to see the crate, falling toward CJ's leg. As the crate fell, CJ's eyes met Kara's and she smiled at him. When the crate hit his foot, when he normally would have yelled and shouted obscenities, he simply smiled back and shed a small tear of pain in his left eye. He could feel the throbbing in his foot, an excruciating pain, and all he did was smile, and shed that simple tear.

Greg shouted, "Dude, are you okay? That looked like it could have broken your ankle!"

When Greg and Kara reached CJ, Kara innocently asked, "Are you okay?"

CJ, grimaced and responded, "My ankle is throbbing with pain, intense pain, but I am okay." he paused, as CJ and Kara looked at each other. Greg remained silent, as he was not sure what the interactions between CJ and Kara were going to be. He had known this rough mechanic long enough to know that he would be respectful of a young child when one was present. CJ then spoke hesitantly through his pain, "You must be Kara, I have heard so much about you."

Kara just smiled.

CJ was still looking directly into Kara's eyes. He did not know for how long, but for him it felt to last for several minutes. His life almost flashed before his eyes, not like people describe near death experiences, though, what he experienced was more of a remembrance. He suddenly saw everything he had done wrong in his life, it was all brought back to his memory, like a tidal wave, hitting him so hard that the tear he had cried in his left eye due to physical pain, just a few short moments before, was now large amounts of tears streaming from both eyes. He saw the things he had done in his life, and he also saw the people who have been hurt by the things that he had done, which was compounded beyond the direct relationship he had with them. All the pain, all the hurt, and all the agony he had caused, all on him and his emotions at once, as he looked into this little girl's eyes. There is nothing he could do but stand there and cry.

As he was crying and seeing all his life's mistakes, he suddenly realized that he wanted to be different. He wanted to be someone people loved, and respected, not hated, and feared. When he had this thought, an overwhelming peace filled his heart and soul. It was like nothing he had ever felt before, he truly felt at that instance that something tangibly changed inside his heart and soul. He later described the change as a rebirth, like some religious people describe baptism or being saved. He never knew exactly what that meant or if this was in any way, the same thing, but what he did know is that all his desires and passions had now changed. He wanted to do good, and only do good to everyone he would come into contact with from that time on.

Greg said, "Hey big man, seriously, are you okay? What is wrong? Do you think your foot is broken?"

CJ turned his head toward Greg, but his eyes stayed fixed on Kara's, and said, "I have never felt this way in my entire life."

"What do you mean?" asked Greg.

"I feel fantastic. I feel relieved. I feel new. I feel good, very good!"

"Uh, you just dropped a 100 pound crate on your leg and you feel good?" Greg said with a surprised tone.

"Greg," CJ continued, "I do not know what just happened, but I want you to know that your daughter, something about her, is beyond ordinary. She is very special. She has a goodness and peace about her that I have never experienced in my life before. In fact, it is the exact opposite of the way my life has been lived. Her very presence near me has made me want to change, to be a better man than I am, to do good to others, and be nice, not mean, but truly nice to everyone I associate with. I don't know what that is, but I feel peace and comfort right now, like I have never before felt. I feel like I just had some sort of transformation, leaving an old life behind and starting a new life with a clean slate."

CJ then pulled his eyes off little Kara and looked at Greg, "Do you have any idea what I'm talking about? Am I making any sense at all?" CJ was sure what he was feeling, but not sure how to communicate his feelings in words.

Greg thought for a moment and said, "CJ, I do not know exactly what you're trying to say, but I do hear sincerity in your voice; and in your voice I hear a change too. I believe what you are saying. Some people have told me when they meet Kara they feel good, but I've never thought more of it than just the way you should feel when you meet a sweet, innocent child. I get the notion, however, that you are saying something more has happened to you just now."

"Yes," CJ responded enthusiastically, "Yes! Something more than just meeting your daughter; whether it is her or something that has happened coincidentally inside me from the accident, I guess I do not know, but I do know for sure that I am different than I was before I met Kara."

Just then, the two men noticed that Kara had sat herself down near CJ's feet and put her hand on his ankle and foot, which had just been struck by the extremely heavy crate. She closed her eyes and put her other hand above the top of her firsthand. As she did, all the pain and throbbing CJ had been feeling in his foot was eased.

CJ looked at Kara and asked her, "What did you just do?"

Little five-year-old Kara simply and innocently asked, "Are you hurt?"

"Well, I was hurting really bad, but I feel much better now. What did you just do?"

Kara did not answer, just looked down at her hands on his foot and ankle.

Then CJ turned to Greg and asked, "What did she just do?"

"I'm not sure. What do you mean?"

"I mean, my foot was throbbing with excruciating pain. It felt like it was legit' broken or shattered, but the second she touched it, the intense pain went away." CJ gave Greg a puzzled look, "Can you explain that?"

"No, no, I can't CJ. I'm glad you're feeling better, but I have no explanation for your pain going away. It may just be a coincidence; maybe your foot has actually lost feeling due to the blow it took, and the resulting swelling. You should have Brian take a look at it"

"Yeah, maybe you're right, I'll do that" CJ then put his hand on Greg's shoulder, something that was out of character for this large, rough and tough man, and said, "but that does not change whatever just happened to me. I feel so much different now. I feel like a new man, like I have never felt before, totally renewed. Thank you for bringing your little girl to go with us this week. I have a good feeling about this trip; I think we will have a successful week."

"I hope you're right brotha. I hope you're right."

Just at that moment, Kara looked up at her father with those big sapphire eyes of hers. She looked at him deeply, and simply smiled. Greg knew at that moment something special had just happened. He did not know to what extent, nor did he know the explanation, but he knew, deep within his soul, that he needed to remember that moment.

"You are someone very special; very, very special," he reached down and picked up his little girl in his arms, and hugged her tightly.

Kara spent most of the rest of the day close to her dad's side, meeting the rest of the crew, and seeing the boat, including the room that she would learn to call her own. It was smaller than her room at home, about 8' x 8'. It had a small bed with a small shelf above it, a little desk and chair and a small closet. There was also some space under the bed to store some belongings. Kara loved it, she felt very special to have her own place on her dad's boat. It was right next to her dad's quarters and below the captain's deck, so she would always know where she could find him.

Greg was a good and thoughtful father and had made a special trip to the store before this voyage in order to get the things he knew Kara would like to have, such as coloring books, pens and crayons, and some new pocket-sized dolls. When Kara opened her desk and saw the new supplies, her eyes widened and lit up like sunshine.

"Thank you daddy!" She exclaimed, "I love it! Thank you for my room and thank you for my new coloring books and the dollies!"

Greg smiled, "You're very welcome sweetheart. You're a good girl and I want this to be a fun trip for you. I want this to be a fun place for you to be when you can come with me."

The rest of the trip was rather ordinary for Greg and his crew. They had success in the usual areas they were used to trolling.

Kara had such a good time. Everyone on the crew went out of their way to make her feel very special, and she certainly did. She felt like the most important person on the boat. Of course, if you ask Greg or any of the other crew, they would all say that she, indeed, was the most important. Whenever any of the crew encountered Kara on the voyage, they would ask her how the trip was going for her and ask if there was anything they could do for her. When Matt would prepare meals, he would always make sure there was something that he thought Kara would like to eat. She always did, she was not a finicky eater like most kids her age.

During the trip, Greg noticed something else very particular about having Kara on board… He noticed that whenever the crew had realized they had full nets, and it was time to hoist them in, Kara would come to the deck and watch. She would not get in the way at all. It was hardly noticeable that she was even there. She would just stand away from the work area where she could see what was going on and just watch. She would watch with very intent eyes; her face would be full of an expression of peace and serenity.

"What do you think she's doing?" the crew would ask each other.

"I have no idea, but it almost looks like she is counting our catch."

"Yeah, it does, but that's kind of impossible, right?"

"That is true, but don't you think it is very weird that she always seems to know when we are about to drag the nets in?"

Then, when the crew had all the catch in the under deck storage area, she would return to her room and get back to her drawing and playing or whatever else she had been doing.

When the Danielle and her crew had completed day four of their typical week long fishing, they had caught a full week's load, so they anchored, cleaned up, and looked forward to heading back first thing in the morning. While Matt was preparing dinner, Kara found Greg and asked if she could get in the water. This was something he did not expect to hear from Kara on her first sail with the crew, but it did not surprise him. He knew she loved the water. He knew she was a great swimmer, even at her young age.

Greg did not know quite what to say to his little girl. Swimming while out on a fishing trip was not something that he, his father, or any of his crew had ever even thought about doing. They were always focused on the work they had to do and getting back to their families. When they had spare time, they would sit around and play cards or tell stories, but never swim.

Greg looked at Kara and asked, "Why do you want to swim out here in the distant sea?"

"I love swimming daddy."

"I know you do honey."

"Look at how pretty the water is," Kara said as if it was obvious to anyone.

Greg looked out at the water, and saw how peaceful and inviting it looked. As he looked, he felt as if he had been taking the beauty of the sea for granted lately, not taking time to recognize its magnificence. He turned to his sweet little girl, and said, "okay, I think that is a great idea. Let's go for a swim!"

"Yippee!" shouted Kara, as she took off her shirt, already in her swimming suit underneath.

Greg and Kara spent some time swimming that evening, just the two of them, while the rest of the crew had dinner and played cards. They laughed and splashed; splashed and laughed. It was a night that Greg will always remember, Kara's first time out on the Danielle and his first time swimming off the bow of his mighty ship.

When they were finished swimming and getting dried off, Kara asked her dad, "Can I go swimming in the morning too?"

Greg looked at her, with those amazing, colorful eyes staring back at him and, without hesitation, simply said, "If you think you can get up before the crew, then okay, we will go swimming."

"I can daddy, I really can? Thank you! I love swimming!"

Then they went back to their cabins, changed their clothes, had some dinner, and then headed off to bed.

Greg informed the crew of Kara's early morning plans so no one would be alarmed.

Kara, even though still very young, had done a significant amount of swimming, but it was that evening, swimming in the wide-open ocean, with her dad, that her love affair with the sea solidified. She loved it. Every second of it.

Something else also started that night, or rather, the next morning. Greg began to have his nightmare; the dramatic dream that would soon become quite routine for him.

It was the very next morning, in the middle of that dream, that he was quickly awakened by the sound of the splash; his precious little girl had jumped into the water to have an early morning swim. Panic, then peace, like nothing he had ever felt before. Nothing he could even describe to anyone. He jumped from bed and ran to the side of the boat just in time to see his daughter bob back up to the surface.

"Good morning daddy!"

"Good morning honey."

"Are you going to swim with me?" Kara asked sincerely

"Not this morning. I have to get some things ready to go. Have fun though, I will be watching you when I can."

"Okay, I will." She said, as she dove down in the water with her feet flipping and splashing at the surface.

Chapter 7 - The Drawing

A couple years later, on one of the Danielle's weekly trips, Kara again joined her father and his crew for a trip out to sea, something she had become very accustomed to doing, especially during the summer months.

It was a beautiful evening on the water; the kind of evening you only see in the summertime. The skies were blue, orange, and red as the sun was slowly dropping toward the horizon. The water was calm, like an undisturbed high-mountain lake in the early morning. It was very rare to have conditions like these, especially in the gulf. As Greg sat at the helm and marveled at the beauty he was fortunate enough to behold at that time, he started thinking to himself that he did not remember nights like these when he was growing up fishing with his dad, nor did he remember nights as beautiful as this when he was working for his dad those long, hard 10 years prior to obtaining his own ship.

It had been another 10 years since he started out on his own with the Danielle; his dad, Robert, had worked with him for the first couple years, and then went to fulfill his lifelong goal of spending every moment of his remaining years with Helen, the love of his life; just as he had promised her.

The more Greg thought about the beauty of the evening, the more he realized that it had only been for the last few years that he could remember nights like the one he was witnessing on this evening. He thought that to be strange and decided to pull up the Internet on his laptop to research weather patterns and determine if there have been any meteorological changes in the earth's atmosphere the last few years, which would explain the beautiful phenomenon he had been experiencing recently.

He went to the national weather center website, and did some searching, but was not able to find anything relating to any of the searches he was looking for. There was no other explanation that he could find. He then went to a few of the Internet blogs for fishermen, both commercial and recreational, specifically for those that fished in the Gulf of Mexico region like him. Although Greg was aware of these Internet blogs, he did not frequent them, because he had always seemed to do just fine with his own knowledge that he and his crew had obtained through the years.

While he was reading some of the blog entries, he started to notice there were a few comments, here, and there, regarding weather phenomena, such as the one he had so often been experiencing the last few years. Some of the blog comments described it almost exactly like Greg would; the sky, blue, orange, and red with the waters, more calm than they could ever imagine. He tried to find some posts like this that were older, but they seemed to only be dated back about three to five years. This was very perplexing to Greg as he was somewhat of an analytical guy. He wanted to know what might be causing this change in the gulf's weather patterns.

As he was thinking about this and reading some more of the Internet blogs, he caught, with the corner of his eye, the sun, just as it was meeting the horizon. He turned his head to look at it, and saw something he had never seen before in his entire life.

"What is that? "He said to himself, "what on earth is that? "

Just as the big orange sun was reaching the horizon, there appeared to be a green light, reaching up from the ocean, venturing about halfway into the sun's circumference. Greg stood up, grabbed his telescope, and walked quickly to the edge of the boat.

He positioned his telescope just right, so he would be able to see the sun as clearly as possible. He looked through the lens, adjusted the focus the best he could and he saw this green light get larger, appearing to take the form of a woman. Greg grabbed the telescope with both hands, pushing his eye against it, as if he wanted to transport himself directly to the image he was seeing. Then he felt something in his heart, it began to swell within him, like the rising tide. It was powerful, it was uncontrollable; it overcame him. He had no choice, but to sit down on the wooden bench near him. He began crying, overcome with emotions he had not felt in years.

"I haven't felt this way since she… " Greg looked around, making sure none of his crew were within earshot of him talking to himself, his tears continued, "I haven't felt this way since before I lost her."

Greg stood back up and walked to the bow, leaning over toward the water, "Oh, baby, I love you! Wherever you are, I love you! I will always love you!" Greg was sobbing as he shouted into the air, "I miss you every second of every day!!"

Then he heard the voice of his little girl. She was singing one of her favorite songs, "God Only Knows," by the Beach Boys. Her grandma Helen had taught her that song and told her it was her favorite song when grandma and grandpa were young:

"I may not always love you
But as long as there are stars above you
You never need to doubt it.
I'll make you so sure about it.
God only knows what I'd be without you.
If you should ever leave me
The life would still go on, believe me.
The world could show nothing to me
So what good would living do me
God only knows what I'd be without you"

Kara loved to sing, and even though she was just a child and her primary audience was a bunch of rough and tough fishermen, they all said she sang like nothing they had ever heard before. Some of them would say it was the sounds of heaven; while others would refer to her as the beautiful voice of the great sea. One thing they all agreed on, though, was the peace they felt when they heard her. It spoke to their soul when she would sing. Regardless of what was troubling them, when Kara would sing, they would immediately become calm and figure out easy solutions to the issues that may have been previously clouding their minds.

Greg wiped the tears from his face and eyes.

The singing got closer, and Greg turned to see Kara as she exited the helm room. Greg clapped his hands together twice, rapidly, and held his arms out in Kara's direction. She knew what that meant and she loved it! Kara started running toward her father and jumped into his arms. He pulled her up to his chest and spun her around and around, smothering her with kisses, carrying her back inside, and then gently tossing her into his cushioned captain's chair. Her smile reached from ear to ear. She absolutely loved her daddy!

"What have you been up to little girl?" Asked Greg, with a grin on his face.

"I have been coloring, daddy." Answered Kara.

Greg noticed that Kara was holding a partially folded piece of coloring paper.

"Oh, really," his grin had turned to more of a smirk, "I don't believe you. You're going to have to prove it to me."

"Okay, I can," said Kara, "just look at this!"

Kara held up the paper she had in her hand for her dad to view. When Greg looked at it, his complexion changed dramatically, he looked pale and stunned, the smile having withdrawn from him. He took a couple stumbling steps backward and bumped into the ship's horn, which made a loud, low, Bello. The picture Kara had drawn looked exactly like the view out the ship's bow that Greg had been marveling over just minutes before.

"What's wrong dad? Don't you like it?"

Greg quickly responded, as tears again began to swell in his eyes, "I love it, honey, I love it! It is one of the most beautiful drawings I have ever seen!"

He showered his precious daughter with compliments about the drawing, but at the same time, thinking about what the connection might be. As he did, he realized that Kara usually colors in her private quarters where there is no porthole for an outside view.

"Kara, honey," Greg knew what he wanted to ask, but was unsure he wanted to hear the answer… so he paused.

"What dad? What's the matter?" Young little Kara was confused by her dad's strange demeanor, which did not seem to match the compliments he was giving about her drawing.

"Honey, where were you drawing tonight? Were you out on the bow?" Greg had been at the helm and bow all evening and had not seen her.

"No, I was coloring in my room like I always do," she responded innocently, but very matter of fact.

Greg suddenly felt that he had made the connection that he was not expecting to make between his daughter's drawing and the scene he had just witnessed. As he did, a great relief consumed him. It was calming and peaceful, like the times long ago when he would hear the sea speaking to him, or the time he chose the name of his ship. He knew that his little Kara was not ordinary, but this was something amazing, even unexplainable.

"Kara," he asked, "what made you decide to draw the sunset the way you did? Do you remember seeing it like that on other days when you have been out with me in the summertime?"

"Is it wrong daddy?"

"No," Greg answered quickly "not at all, I love what you have drawn. In fact, it's hard to describe how much I love it; I am just wondering where you got the idea to draw it like you did if you were in your room and not looking at the sunset tonight."

"Daddy," Kara spoke softly, "do you know how you always tell me I was born of the sea?"

Greg nodded, "yes, my little sea princess. You were born of the sea, that's what I always say."

"Well," Kara explained, "When you tell me that I was born of the sea, this drawing is what I see in my head, and when I am feeling lonely, wishing I had a friend to play with, I think about what you say to me and this is what I see in my head and then I can see it outside too."

With her sweet innocence, she did not even realize what she was saying may mean that the weather would change to match her thoughts. Most fathers would dismiss a child, saying such a thing, or rationalize some other explanation for what his daughter was explaining, but not Greg. He had seen and experienced far too many amazing, miraculous things, both in his life and with his daughter, to doubt his little girl, so he simply responded in the most kind, loving way he could muster up, "that is perfect Kara, absolutely perfect! Just like you!"

Kara backed up, then ran and jumped in her dad's big arms, one more time and they hugged, smiled, and smothered each other with kisses once more.

"I love you so much, honey!" Greg said to Kara, "you are daddy's little angel, did you know that?"

Greg's heart was filled with joy, stronger than it had been in years. He then reflected again on the thoughts of his wife he had been having earlier, realizing that he had not felt this good since the night Kara was born; the night he lost his wife and gained a daughter. The worst, best day of his life.

"I know, daddy, you always tell me that," Kara responded, once again, smiling from ear to ear. "I love you too, daddy, and so does the sea, my mommy."

"What? What did you say?" Greg wasn't quite sure what Kara was saying, but he did not want to alarm her again by sounding too surprised at what she had said, so he simply and softly said "what do you mean by that?"

Greg had been telling Kara her whole life that she was born of the sea, but this was the first time Kara had brought it up and she said to her father again, "the sea loves you daddy. When I am singing to myself, or thinking about mommy, or sometimes, when I dream, I can hear a voice that I know is her telling me that she loves me and she loves you. And will always be with us, watching over us to keep us safe."

"You are right honey, you are very right!" Greg said to his little daughter, with great joy in his voice, "your mother does love you very much, and will always be looking over you and I know she loves me. She promised me that she would love me forever, through all time, and I promised her the same. I hope you can feel her love for you and I, as much as you can feel the love I give to you."

Kara snuggled in a little tighter to her dad's hug and said, "I do daddy, I do."

Greg was so happy at that moment. He thought to himself that he had not been so happy since the days he had with his sweet wife, and he wondered if now was the time that he should tell Kara more about her mother. He wanted to tell her everything and his heart swelled within him, and then he heard a voice he was very familiar with, speaking to his heart and mind, Saying, "not yet, Greg, not yet. She is still too young."

Greg immediately felt extreme peace come over him and could feel the peace covering Kara as well and he knew that everything was understood between the two of them right now; the way it needed to be at this time in her life. They sat and held each other for a few minutes. Greg, knowing that this was one of those times that they had drawn closer together, and understood each other only as a father and a daughter could.

"It's time to get you ready for bed, little girl," Greg said, "go get your jammies on and brush your teeth and I will be down to tuck you in, in a few minutes."

"Okay daddy," she said, as she gave him a kiss on the cheek. Then she jumped off his lap and headed down to her room.

Greg didn't move much for the next five minutes. He just sat, pondering the things he had just experienced with his daughter, grateful that it was a peaceful night. He was grateful his crew was content, grateful his business was doing well, grateful he had lived and is still living a life he could have never dreamed would bring him so much peace and happiness.

From the lower deck, he heard that sweet little voice of his daughter again, "Dad, I'm ready to be tucked in."

He smiled and said loudly, but gently, "okay, I'll be there in a minute."

Greg went to the little stairway that led to the galley below, walked down, and turned into Kara's little room, where he saw that she had taped her drawing on the ceiling right above her bed.

"That's a good place for your drawing."

"I wanted it to be the last thing I saw before going to sleep after you tuck me in at night. It makes me so happy; I just know it will help me sleep well!"

"I think it will, too, sweetheart, I think it will, too." Greg was now sitting on the side of Kara's little bed and asked, "do you want me to sing your song to you or read or tell you a story?"

"My song, my song!" She answered quickly and decisively.

"Okay honey," Greg said, with a soft, gentle voice, "your Mom came up with this song before you were born. She knew you were going to be a little girl, even before the doctors could tell us, and she knew what your name would be…"

"Kara Danielle Landers, your name's a legacy
Of love and faith and honest work, the way your life should be.
So live your life for others, love and laugh along the way.
Do this, my dear, and I promise you, your dreams will come true someday."

Greg had sung this little song to Kara many, many times before, and every time he did, they felt closer together, as if unified by the memory of his wife and Kara's mother, Danielle. They both missed her so much, but felt that she was so close to them when he would sing this song. It was one of the most valued treasures they had together.

Greg remembered a few years back, when Kara was just starting to understand life, language, and family relationships. She asked Greg why her middle name was the same as his boat, which took him off guard at the time. He had always told her she was born of the sea, but knew he would need to tell her more, so when she asked about her name, at just three years old, he told her Danielle was her mother's name too. He told her the boat was named after her mother, and she wanted Kara to have her name as well. It was as if she knew that she would be passing on much of her personality to her little girl. She named her and Greg knew it was important at that time to make sure Kara, for the rest of her life, knew that her name came from her mom.

It was also at that time when Greg first tried to explain to Kara that her mother had been gone since she was born. It was very difficult to explain to a three-year-old, so he just told her, as simply as he could. He told Kara that when she was born her mother saw and held her for a few minutes, and then was taken by the sea. From that day on, he continued to tell Kara she was born of the sea, and would rehearse the same story whenever the topic would be brought up by her. He wanted, so much, to tell her more about her mother, but knew that the time had not yet come.

As Greg was thinking about these special memories, he kissed Kara on the forehead and took her hand, like a gentleman takes a lady, and kissed her on the hand as well. This was a special routine they had, Kara then looked at her Daddys big, rough, fisherman hand, and kissed him right back, right on the back of the hand as he had done with her.

"Good night, sweetie," he said, "sleep good, I love you."

"Good night daddy, I love you too." Kara then pulled her blanket just a little tighter and rolled over to her side to fall asleep.

Greg shut the door, paused in the hall, and said a little prayer. He always wanted to make sure his God knew how grateful he was to Him for blessing his life with such a wonderful, beautiful daughter. He then returned to his helm room to complete his logbooks for the day, and write in his journal about the personal and business events of the day.

Chapter 8 - Something is Wrong with My Legs

It was a beautiful, late summer evening. It was the weekend. The whole Landers family, Greg, Kara, Jeff, Courtney, Robert, and Helen had spent most of the day out on the Gulf, just relaxing, enjoying some sun, playing in the water, and doing some recreational fishing on one of their family leisure boats. The boys, although they were professional fisherman, still loved to go out together when occasion permitted to try to catch some gamefish, most of the time catch and release. They liked to try and catch a variety of fish, always looking for something bigger and more beautiful. They really loved sea creatures; Robert even had the belief that one day he would find an unidentified species, and be able to name it himself, but had yet to do so.

"I love the weather of today," said Kara to her grandma while they were finishing up some barbecued flounder for dinner.

"What do you love about it sweetheart?" Helen asked.

Kara explained, "I love to see the sun, full and bright. I like the way it makes the water look clear and blue, like you can see all the way to the bottom."

"I love that too, Kara," Helen said, "I always wonder if there is life down there that we do not know of."

Kara did not think much of what Helen said, and replied, "like the fish grandpa is looking for?"

"Yes, something like that."

It was getting to be late in the day and Kara had spent most of the time swimming. The sun was beginning to set on the west sea and Kara asked if she could do just a little bit more swimming.

"Of course you can," Greg told her, "don't swim too far away from the boat, okay?"

Kara was already in the air diving off the side of the boat as she yelled back at her dad, "I won't daddy."

"Courtney!" Yelled, Kara, "come for a swim with me."

"I'll be in in a few minutes if you promise to go slow!" Courtney replied.

"Okay, come on!" Then Kara turned and swam under the water for a few seconds.

Courtney and Kara swam for about the next 30 minutes until Courtney told her she was getting tired and returned to the boat. "It's almost dark," she said, "you should come in soon too."

"Just a few more minutes and I will," Kara said with a smile, water streaming down her face and hair.

While Kara enjoyed her final evening swim, Greg, Jeff, and Robert were busy cleaning up and stowing their fishing equipment while Helen and Courtney were talking and cleaning up the food and other items from the day. None of them even noticed Kara come in from the water.

When the men had finished, Greg said, "Mom, Courtney, have you seen Kara? Is she still out there?"

It was now dark and he did not like Kara swimming by herself when it was dark.

"Kara," he yelled over the side of the boat, "are you still out there?"

There was no response.

"Kara!" He yelled louder this time, "where are you? Are you okay?"

When he stopped to listen, the rest of the family had quieted as well. Then Greg heard Kara's soft little voice, through whimpering and tears. "I'm over here Dad."

Greg turned around and saw Kara in the back corner of the boat, sitting behind some fishing gear. He went over to her as the rest of the family gathered around her too.

"What's the matter honey? Why didn't you answer me when I was calling you?" Greg said as he sat down next to her.

Kara's eyes were full of tears, and she continued crying and whimpering softly.

"You scared us all honey, we didn't know what had happened to you," Greg said with concern.

Kara still did not say anything in response to her dad's questions. He could see that something was definitely troubling her or was painful to her.

"Did something happen out in the water?" His questions continued, "Did something attack you? Did you get hurt? What is it sweetie?"

"You can tell us, honey, it's all right," Helen said, lovingly, adding her concern to the minor inquisition.

Kara began to speak, very softly, "I don't know what happened, but I think there is something wrong with me."

Greg's fatherly instinct kicked in and he immediately began asking more questions, "Are you sick? Are you hurt? What do you mean something is wrong with you?"

Helen touched Greg on the shoulder and said, "Just let her tell us, it is apparent she is not terribly hurt, just let her have a chance to talk."

"What is it Kara?" Helen asked.

"There's something wrong with my legs," she said quietly.

"What? What do you mean?"

Kara's tears had mostly subsided, but she was still slightly whimpering, which caused her to speak slowly and bumpy.

"Well," she paused and sniffled, "I was swimming like I always do and something happened to my legs."

Greg began to ask another question, but Helen patted him on the shoulder again, and just said, "let her finish."

"I was swimming and kicking through the water like I always do when I felt my knees start to bend the wrong way."

"Did it hurt?" Courtney asked.

"Yeah, what do you mean your knees bent the wrong way?" Greg added to Courtney's question.

Kara had been sitting in a crouched position, having pulled her knees into her chest. She removed her arms from holding her legs and straightened them out in front of her, putting her legs flat on the boat deck. Then she reached forward, put one hand on her left knee and grabbed her left foot with the other hand and lifted up her foot. Her heel came nearly 10 inches off the deck, while her knee remained flat.

"Whoa," said Jeff, "that's intense!"

Kara then demonstrated the same thing with the other leg and simply asked, "What's wrong with me?"

Greg responded, "Does it hurt?"

"No, it doesn't hurt at all."

"Well, Honey," Greg said, with a smile, "I am a fisherman, not a doctor, but I'm pretty sure you're double jointed."

"What's that?" Kara asked innocently.

"It isn't bad, it just means that your knees have an extra part, more than most people do. It means that you can bend your knee the wrong way, like you just showed us."

"Are other people like this?" Kara asked inquisitively.

Greg looked at Helen, who responded to the question, "Some people are, but not very many. You are very special to have double jointed knees. It will really help you swim better and faster when you learn to use it the right way."

"What do you mean grandma?" Kara asked, her tears all cleared up and beginning to sound happy again.

Helen lifted up her sundress just above her knees and said, "Grandma is going to show you something."

Helen put most of her weight on one of her legs and bent it backward about 3 inches, and then she repeated the same thing with the other leg, then back-and-forth.

"You are double jointed too!?" Kara was very excited now, "will you show me how to swim faster? I know what a good swimmer you are Grammy!"

"I will show you what I know and then you can learn what works for you to be the best swimmer you can be," Helen said with a grin.

"That's cool grandma. I thought something was wrong with me."

"Turns out there's something wrong with both of you," Robert said sarcastically.

They all laughed as Greg picked up Kara and gave her a big hug and whispered in her ear, "You are amazing Kara, simply amazing. I love you so much!"

Chapter 9 - Uncle Jeff

Kara's years as a child growing up were spent, most of the time with her Dad on his boat, out on the sea fishing and swimming. That is, if it was summer, when she was not in school. When it was not summer, during the nine months of the year she needed to be at school, she lived with her uncle Jeff and his wife Courtney.

Jeff had grown up working with Greg on the fishing boat during the summer months, but not nearly as much as Greg. Jeff just did not have the same desire and passion that Greg had. Jeff appreciated what his Father did for him and how hard he worked for the family, but he was drawn in a different direction from a young age.

When Jeff was just a boy at about six years old, one of his friends, Ryan, took him out with his dad to ride motorcycles. Ryan's Dad had a spare bike just his size, a small 50 cc dirt bike with just a few gears and a top speed of about 35 mph. It was very safe for young kids to learn to ride. They went to an area outside of town with a lot of open space, well marked trails, and un-crowded dirt roads.

When Jeff got on the bike for the first time, Ryan showed him a couple things about how to operate it and Ryan's Dad made sure he had a helmet on and told him to take it easy and be careful, ensuring young Jeff that he would be close nearby to help him if he needed it. Jeff revved the little engine, popped the clutch, and forgot to lift his feet off the ground which caused him to slide to the back of the seat, shifting the weight to the rear of the bike as he accelerated. As a result Jeff found himself with the front wheel of that little bike in the air, and his only reaction was to give it more throttle. This, of course, made the wheely action greater and he ended up on his butt on the ground with the bike going all the way over, the handle bars hitting the ground right in front of him.

Ryan and his Dad burst out laughing, they figured he was okay because they had both done about the same thing the first time on a dirtbike. They laughed and laughed while they ran over to make sure Jeff was indeed okay.

"Nice one Jeff," said Ryan through his laughter.

"Was that supposed to happen?" asked Jeff, sincerely not knowing if he had done something wrong or not, "did I break it?"

"The bike is fine," said Ryan's dad. "It is a little bike meant to take a beating and be wrecked a lot. My boy here did just about the same thing when he rode it for the first time. It was just as funny then. He didn't think so, just like your feeling now, but you'll be fine too, and be able to laugh about it later. It's all part of the learning process."

"Yeah, my Dad always says if you don't ever fall down, you never get any better at riding," Ryan said, feeling like he was an expert rider at this young stage in his life.

"I crash all the time!' Ryan continued, as if he was proud of it.

"So, you okay?" asked Ryan's Dad, "Do you want to keep riding?"

"That was kind of fun," Jeff said, trying his best to be brave, smiling while trying to hide that his ego and his butt were both hurting.

He went over to the bike, which had been picked up and straightened out by Ryan's Dad, got back on and gave it another try. This time, having quickly learned his lesson, leaned forward as he took off and made sure he got his feet to the foot pegs as he was accelerating. Off he went, kicking up rocks and dirt.

Because this was his first time riding, he was not totally comfortable with the bike yet, so he just went back and forth a few times, following his friend, who was kindly going slow and showing him how to turn, leaning as he did, just like riding a bicycle.

After about an hour and a half, Jeff had learned it quite well and was riding nearly as good as Ryan.

Then Jeff started taking the lead, "Let's go over there!" He shouted, as he spun the rear wheel, turned, and took off to a hill in the nearby area.

When they got there, Jeff noticed that there were more trails, up and down the hills, in and out of tree and shrub areas, and over bumps and jumps.

Jeff stopped and said to his friend, "This is so cool, have you ridden here before?"

"Not very much, but my dad does all the time," replied Ryan, trying to sound proud of his Dad.

"Do you wanna?"

"Do you?"

Both boys were trying to be brave and adventurous, knowing that some of the trail jumps looked big and scary, but not wanting the other boy to think that they were scared.

"I will, if you will," Jeff said in a daring tone.

The two young boys stared each other down, just for a moment, and then Ryan revved his little engine, popped his clutch, spinning his rear wheel, and took off up the closest trail.

Not to be out done, Jeff followed, keeping close behind his friend, as he wound back-and-forth, in and out of the trees, up and down the bumps. They would ride as fast as they could, then slow down for the curves and jumps. Jeff was having more fun than he could ever remember, then he passed his friend on a straight trail down a hill with a bump at the bottom of it about 5 feet high.

Ryan tried to yell at him to slow down, "You're going to fast for that jump, Jeff! You're gonna crash!"

Jeff did not hear him. He was feeling something his six year old body never felt before, adrenaline, pure and strong. He felt invincible as he approached the bottom of that jump, going just as fast as he could go. By this time, Ryan had stopped his bike to watch what was about to happen, expecting only the worst results. He had jumped before and crashed a lot doing it. Also at that very moment, Ryan's dad was approaching the hill area they had been riding and saw what was about to happen. He also stopped his bike to watch, feeling somewhat helpless.

Jeff hit that jump and was launched into the air like a big steel ball out of an old warship cannon. He was unfamiliar with what to do to position himself and the bike properly as he took off or landed, but he still executed it as though he had done it many times.

Up, up in the air he flew; for what felt to him as hundreds of feet for several minutes, suspended weightless, but was actually only about 6 feet in the air for a few seconds. Jeff felt every molecule of air rushing into his helmet and passing through his lungs; it swept around his arms and body, and through his legs as he stood up on the foot pegs to approach the landing. He came down just at the bottom of the other side of the little hill and stomped on his foot brake and slid the locked rear wheel to the right as he leaned into a left-hand turn to a stop. Dirt was kicking up, dust all around him, and he was, for a moment, in a cloud of it. As the dust settled, Ryan and his Dad came riding over to him, laughing and shouting with adoration.

"Holy crap!" Ryan shouted "You are crazy!"

"That was awesome," Jeff responded, shouting, right back at them, "Did you see how high I flew? It was like I was a superhero!"

The three of them talked and reveled in the moment for a while and continued their day of riding, Jeff hitting as many jumps as he could find, continually trying to find one bigger and better than the previous. He was fearless that day.

All the way home that evening and through many other days to follow, those two boys talked about that day and how much fun it was.

When Jeff got home, he told his parents and Greg all about it. They listened to his story with excitement for him, happy that he had fun.

Greg tried to discount what his brother was saying, "I bet it wasn't as big as you say." Which was true, of course, but that's just how boys are sometimes.

"Be nice and listen to your brother's story," Robert told him.

"Can I have a motorcycle?" Jeff asked.

"Now Jeff," Robert said with care, "we are very glad you had fun today, and we are very glad you made it home alive, but we just don't have the money to get you a motorbike."

"I'm sorry, honey," Helen added.

"Even if we did, who would take care of it, who would take you out riding?" Robert didn't realize he was setting himself up for a response. Jeff was ready for it, even at his young age of six.

"I will take care of it!" Jeff exclaimed, "and Ryan's dad said he would help me and that I could go riding with them anytime I want."

Robert and Helen looked at each other and smiled.

Then Robert looked at Jeff and said, "Jeff, we think it is important for you to have responsibilities as you grow up, that is one of the reasons I have you and Greg go with me on the boat to help out sometimes. So if you think it is something you really want to do, your mom and I will support you in getting a bike for yourself."

Robert and Helen did not want to diminish his desires at this time, and as young as Jeff still was, they did not really think he was totally serious about his plan. They thought of the situation similar to when a child brings home a puppy or a kitty they found and begs to keep it; then only a few days later, they realize how difficult it is to take care of, and abandon the idea. It's sad, but true.

"I am going to work very hard, and save every penny until I have enough money!" Jeff said with some fortitude uncommon for a boy his age, "Mom, is there anything I can do for you right now to earn some money?"

This would prove to be quite the task over the next few years, but he never let go of his desire to have a bike of his own. When Greg would talk about how awesome it was to go out fishing with Dad and his crew, Jeff would be talking about riding. Jeff would go out with Ryan every chance he could, riding one of their older bikes. He continued to develop his skills as a rider.

Finally, when he was almost 12 years old, he had enough money to buy a bike that he wanted. He was much bigger now, and could handle a lot more power than he could when he was younger. With his Dad, Ryan, and Ryan's Dad, he went out shopping for a new dirt bike, or at least new to him. Robert had talked to him about the value, risks, and rewards of buying a brand new bike versus trying to find something used. Jeff was fine with trying to find a nice used bike and was glad to have the help of his friend's Dad, who to Jeff, was the local expert on everything dirt bike related.

After a weekend of looking, they found the perfect bike for Jeff. It was a 125cc former motocross bike, used by a rich kid only a few times. The kid's Dad had bought it for him a couple years ago because his son said he wanted to be a racer, but that only lasted one race and then he quit when he came in dead last and quickly gave up on that idea. They were able to negotiate a price that Jeff could afford and he beamed from ear to ear as they loaded it into the back of Robert's truck and took it home.

On the way home, Ryan's dad said, "You're welcome to keep your bike in our garage."

Jeff did not want to have his new bike that far away from him, even though they live just a mile away from each other. "That's okay thanks, I would rather just push it along the sidewalk to your house whenever we go out."

And that is just what he did, nearly every weekend and some days after school for the next few years.

Four years later, Jeff was known throughout the lower half of the state of Texas as the rider to beat in the youth, 125cc class motocross. He was an amazing rider, already having signed a local dirt bike dealer to sponsor him. He rode every chance he could, getting faster each time, jumping higher over each jump. He had even started doing aerial tricks when he was jumping. This scared his parents and they insisted that he made sure to always have the proper support with him should anything happen to him by accident.

Jeff no longer had any interest in going out on the boat with Greg and their dad. That bugged Greg sometimes, but he was also glad to have the time with his father all to himself to learn the trade he was so passionate about. Greg did like to go watch his brother race, however, because he thought it was pretty cool.

When Jeff was in high school as a senior, he had a serious discussion with his parents about what he wanted to do with his future.

"Mom, dad, I want to go pro," Jeff just blurted it out right in the middle of dinner. It wasn't much of a surprise, though, the thought of Jeff racing motocross professionally had been on their minds a lot. He was very good.

Helen responded quietly, "What does that mean exactly?"

"Well," Jeff paused, "it means I want to ride full-time and make my living doing it."

"Yes, I know what going pro means," said Helen, trying not to be frustrated with her son, not frustrated because of what he wanted with his life, just frustrated because it scared her some. "What are your specific plans? Financing? Sponsorship? What are your plans for money if you do not win?"

Jeff was still a kid, he wanted to race because he loved it and felt the excitement. Every time he was on his bike, every time he was racing.

"I don't know, Mom. Maybe I could go to the community college and get some training on motorcycle repair or something. I could work on motorcycles when I'm not racing, just to make sure I have something that brings in some regular income."

"That is actually a good idea," said Robert, "the community college is a great way to get some training and certifications."

"I'll be honest, Mom and Dad; I have talked to my current sponsor, Mike's bikes, about working for him and racing more. Mike said he would be happy to help me find some bigger sponsors, when I am ready. He thinks I have enough skill to win on the national level. He said we just need to get into some of the bigger regional races to start getting noticed."

"Wow, you really have been thinking about this seriously, haven't you?" Robert asked with a grin of pride on his face.

"Yes, Dad, I really feel like this is what I want to do. You know how much I love to ride and you have seen me, you know that I am good."

"That's true. You are very good, very, very good."

Five years later, Jeff was ranked top five in the country for motocross racing. He had huge national sponsors, and although he had been working as a mechanic full-time originally, he no longer needed to, and just worked on his bikes with his team. He was also engaged to be married to Courtney, his high school girlfriend. The life he had imagined as a kid was becoming his reality.

Chapter 10 - Kara can ride!

Over the years, Kara had become very comfortable at Jeff and Courtney's house. She considered it her home. Of course, her Dad's house was also her home, she felt just as loved and just as cared for at both places.

Each week during the school year, Greg would take Kara to Jeff's house on Sunday evening, have dinner with them, play some games or watch a movie, help Kara get ready for bed, and get her in bed before he would leave to go to his house. There were times that he would stay the night at Jeff's, but because he had to get up very early, he usually didn't want to risk waking anyone else.

Every week, when Greg would tuck his daughter in, they would say "I love you," to each other and then Kara would whisper in her Dad's ear, "You're going to come back, right?"

Greg would always answer by saying the same thing, "You know I am, honey, the biggest, fiercest, strongest sea creatures and storms could not keep me from returning back to you. Sleep good, girl, I'll see you soon."

Even though it was hard for them to be apart, they both loved this little ritual.

"How was your breakfast Kara?" Asked Jeff on a spring Saturday morning.

"Fine," she said quietly.

"That's it, just fine?"Jeff sensed something was on Kara's mind, "I thought biscuits and gravy was one of your favorites."

"It is. It's pretty good."

Jeff and Courtney looked at each other and grinned, knowing that Kara wanted them to inquire about whatever it was on her mind.

"What's the matter, honey?" Courtney asked sweetly.

There was a long pause, "It's okay, Kara, you can talk to us, you know that," Courtney was trying to encourage her. They felt comfortable with each other most of the time. Kara had been spending weekdays with her aunt and uncle during the school year for the past three years. She was now eight years old. Prior to that, she primarily stayed with her Grandparents while Greg was out at sea.

"I wonder when I can learn to ride a dirt bike," Kara spoke quietly.

Jeff laughed out loud, not in a way that he was laughing at her; it was a laugh of joy, surprise, and excitement, like he just got some unexpected great news he had been waiting for, but never really expected to receive.

"You want to ride with me," asked Jeff, "why haven't you ever asked before?"

"I don't know, I guess I didn't know if I could, but I want to see what it is like to ride a dirt bike. I think it is so cool what you do," Kara was speaking more loudly, and clearly now, more confident about discussing this with Jeff.

"Really?" Jeff asked, still sounding surprised

"Yeah, don't you believe me?" said Kara.

"Of course I believe you, Kara. I think it is awesome that you want to learn to ride. I just never thought about it. I had no idea you might be interested in it," Jeff was nearly laughing with joy as he spoke.

"So will you teach me?" Kara was speaking even more excitedly now, anticipating a positive answer.

"Of course I will, Kara. Do you want to come with me today?"

"Really?" She responded as she twirled around on her feet in a circle, expressing her excitement.

"Yeah, don't YOU believe ME?"Jeff said whimsically.

Kara smiled a huge smile and just simply and quietly said, "Yes! " As she gave a little gesture to her side, with her hand in a fist, a solo fist bump of sorts.

"Finish that breakfast already girl!" said Jeff with a tease in his voice, "The trails await you."

Kara ate the rest of her biscuits and gravy faster than she ever had before. Then she ran off to her room to change into some older clothes, long pants, long sleeve shirt, and some old shoes that still fit her okay.

"What should I bring?" She hollered down the hallway to her uncle.

"Just get dressed in old clothes and I will get the rest for you. Courtney is packing us some food to eat," he hollered back.

"What kind of sandwich do you want, Kara?" Her aunt called out.

"Whatever Jeff is having," Kara was nearly singing her response as the excitement in her voice and demeanor increased.

She finished getting ready and ran down the hallway to the kitchen, propelling herself off the corner of the couch, and jumping in the air as she went by. All the way down the hall she was making engine noises, pretending she was a motorcycle rider. She was so excited!

"Where is Jeff?" She asked her aunt as she was finishing up the lunch pack.

"He is out back, loading the bikes and getting the little one running for you."

"It doesn't run?" Kara asked with wonder.

"Of course it does, and very well for as old as it is. Your uncle takes very good care of his bikes; they are all in great shape. I meant he just hasn't had that one out of the shed for a while, so I'm sure he is just double checking that it will be great for you to ride," Courtney wanted to ensure Kara was feeling safe and confident in the dirt bike she would be riding.

"Awesome!" Kara sang out, loudly and prolongedly, something she had heard her uncle do from time to time when he got good news or was enthusiastic about something.

Courtney laughed with her and extended her hand for a fist bump.

Just a few minutes passed by, but it seemed like a lot longer to Kara, and Jeff yelled into the house, "You coming or what?"

Kara, let out a little shriek and said, "I'm coming, I'm coming!"

They both climbed into Jeff's truck and off they went toward the trail area Jeff rode at most often. Just north of where they lived, there was an area around a couple small lakes, with a lot of dirt roads and trails where Jeff liked to go to do his recreational riding. It was only about an hour drive, but today to Kara, it seemed to be taking an eternity. After just 10 minutes on the road, she said to Jeff, "How far is it? This is taking forever."

"Well, somebody is certainly excited today. It's about an hour drive," he said, looking at her with a smile through the rear view mirror.

"Is that long, medium, or short?" Kara asked.

Jeff laughed and said, "Good question. I guess the best way to answer that is…" he thought for a few seconds, and remembered how much she loved watching her favorite television show, sea stories, "I guess it's about three sea stories episodes. Do you want to put on something to watch? Is the DVD case in the back of the seat?"

"Ya." Kara looked for her favorite sea stories video. It was, indeed, her favorite thing to watch, and put it in the overhead DVD player. Before she knew it, they were at the parking area to unload the bikes.

Jeff took care of getting the bikes ready and set Kara up with some knee pads, elbow pads, and a helmet with goggles. The helmet was a little too big, and she looked a bit like an olive on a toothpick. They both laughed a little about it, but it was still safe. Jeff gave her some simple instructions about turning, shifting, accelerating, and braking.

"Do you think you are ready to give it a try?" He asked.

Without even answering him, she flipped out the kickstart lever with her foot, stood up, and gave it a step down while turning the accelerator just enough to get the little engine to rev up and get started. Just that easy, she stepped on the gearshift, leaned forward, and popped the clutch. Then off she went, kicking up dirt and dust all over Jeff as she took off, as if she had been riding for years.

Jeff just laughed out loud and watched as she went down the trail, shifting from gear to gear until she was at what appeared to him to be the little bike's top speed. She then hit the brake, skidding to a turning slide, while downshifting. She then slightly accelerated through the turn, spinning the rear wheel with perfect balance, in order to speed back in Jeff's direction.

Jeff couldn't believe what he was seeing. She looked like he did after he had been riding for several years!

"What kind of a little girl jumps on a dirt bike for the first time and rides like that?" He thought to himself as she rode toward him, a little too fast for him to feel comfortable. He raised his hand and gave her a slow down signal, but she did not slow down. She just continued right at him and just about 25 feet from where he was standing, she hit her brakes, again skidding the rear wheel and shifting down at the same time. This time, when she was almost stopped, she put her leg down, turned to the left and accelerated, spinning that little bike in circles, kicking up as much dirt and dust as she could for about five revolutions.

When she came to a stop, and the dust began to settle, she reached up and yanked off her helmet, let it fall to the ground, and raised both her arms, high above her head, and yelled as loud as she could, "That was totally awesome! Now all I need is a Revved Up!"

That was the exact routine and phrase that Jeff performed at the end of his races. He was under contract to do that, for his biggest sponsor, Revved Up, which was an all natural energy drink company.

Jeff burst out laughing, "That was totally awesome, Kara! Where did you learn to ride like that?" but before she had a chance to answer, he re-phrased the question, "A better question... When did you learn to ride like that?"

"What do you think I do with Courtney at your races? I have been watching you. You taught me everything I just did. You do it every race. You're the best there is! " Kara was nearly shouting with excitement.

"Ha, ha, ha!" Jeff shook his head in total disbelief and amazement at what he just saw. He did not have anything else to say, except, "well then, let's get to some more riding, the day is just getting started!"

They rode together the rest of the day, only stopping for lunch. Kara went everywhere Jeff took her without hesitation and matched all his moves, just slower, except for the jumps. She went over all the jumps, but Jeff was very strict to her that she did not try any of the aerial tricks he had mastered over the many years he had been competing as a professional.

She was fine with that, but without fear or signs of hesitation, she asked him at the end of the day, "Will you teach me some more? I want to ride bigger, faster bikes. I want to learn some of the jumps you do."

"Of course I will! I am so glad you like it, and seriously, I have never seen any first time rider like you. That was so cool! I will take you out whenever I can."

The two of them cleaned up their gear and got it loaded into the truck for the drive home.

"Thanks for taking me, uncle Jeff!" Kara said with a smile.

"You bet, sweetie."

There was not much more said between the two of them for the next few minutes of the drive, until Jeff spoke up, "However, we still need to run this past your dad, but I think he will be okay with it. Especially when I describe what an excellent rider you are."

There was no response from Kara, so Jeff turned his head around to see that she had fallen asleep. He looked forward again and adjusted his rear view mirror so he could see her. She had a dusty goggle outline on her face and had fallen asleep with a grin. She looked so exhausted, but happy too.

"What an amazing kid," he thought to himself, "who would've ever guessed that sweet as all get out little girl could ride a bike like that."

When Jeff could see that she was sound asleep, he pulled the car over to the side of the road and sent a text message to Courtney, Greg, and their parents.

It simply read, "KARA CAN RIDE!"

Chapter 11 - Road Trip

Jeff and Kara arrived home just after sunset and Jeff carried Kara into the house. Courtney helped her get cleaned up and ready for bed while Jeff went back outside to clean up the bikes and equipment. After getting the bikes stored away, he was parking the trailer when he received a call from Greg, who was just getting into cell phone range after a long week at sea.

"What do you mean Kara can ride?" Greg asked hastily.

"I mean she can ride, your daughter is an excellent dirt bike rider," answered Jeff, almost sarcastically, he knew Greg knew what he meant, but may not be on board with it.

"Did you take her to the trails?" assumed Greg.

"Yeah, dude, she did great! You would have loved it!" Jeff said, as convincingly as possible.

"Jeff, you should've checked with me on this. I don't want her to ride dirt bikes. Especially at her young age," Greg's tone was slightly elevated.

"Why not?" Jeff asked, "You know I'll take good care of her and make sure she's safe."

"Even though you would try, it's still dangerous, and I want her to just concentrate on her swimming. She loves swimming!" Greg was also being as convincing as possible.

"Greg, you know I totally respect your decisions as her father, and if you really don't want her to ride, I will understand. But brotha, you have to see her ride first. You won't believe how good she is. It's like she has always been riding. She has such awesome balance. You really, really have to see her ride!" Jeff's tone was very excited!.

"Jeff, I believe that she can ride. She is a very quick learner with everything she tries. I just don't want her to ride. Riding and racing is dangerous; it's not the right environment for a little girl. You never know where she might run into some danger. I just don't think I could handle the worry of not knowing when an accident might happen," Greg said sternly.

There was silence on the phone for about 20 seconds, while the two brothers thought about the conversation.

The silence was broken by Jeff, "Hey man, I know the dangers of the sport. I face it every damn day; every time I am practicing, and then even more on race day with the other riders. I get it." After a short pause, Jeff continued, "I have been very lucky to have had a career this long and not have had any major accidents. I think about that all the time. It terrifies

Courtney to think about it. We used to fight about it all the time, until she decided to accept what the reality is, which is that there is a danger in the sport, and an accident is likely to happen. She decided that she could not afford to worry about it all the time anymore. She made the decision to just watch, support me, and understand that if, and frankly probably when, something does happen, we will cross that bridge at the time."

After another brief pause, Jeff said more, as his voice became very somber, "You know, as well as I do, that there are dangers everywhere. There are dangers at school, in the pool, and especially in the ocean, her favorite place to swim."

Greg took a few moments to gather his thoughts and said, "I didn't mean to open up some difficult emotions with you, Jeff, I just want Kara to be safe."

"I know, no worries. I am not saying she should be a racer or anything, she is only eight years old, but she loved it; she totally loved it! You should really come out with us next week and check it out. Maybe we could just keep it as leisure riding for her if that is what you want. I agree that she is an amazing swimmer and could easily be competitive in the pool when she is older. Just come with us next week out to the trails and see what I'm talking about, okay?"

Greg could sense the passion in Jeff's voice.

"Well, I guess it would be fun to come riding with you. It's been a while and maybe it could be something we could all do together as an activity. I just never thought of it that way. I mean, I never even imagined my sweet little girl riding a motorcycle," Greg laughed as he was much more calm about the idea than he had been at the onset of his call to his brother.

"Oh, wait," Jeff, just had a thought and changed the direction of the plan, "I have a race up in Dallas next weekend, so we can't go riding next week, but why don't you and Kara come with Courtney and I? She sees a lot of the smaller races around here, but it might be fun to go see a race that is much bigger, and will even be televised."

Jeff paused to give Greg a chance to think about it, and said, "What do you say, bro, you in? "

"That actually sounds pretty good. We could use a little road trip and I bet my crew would love to cut our sea voyage short a couple days next week. Things have been going quite well, so I think we could manage that," Greg paused, "let's do it!"

A few hours later, Greg arrived at Jeff's home. It had been a long week and he wanted to bring Kara home before morning. He quietly snuck into her room and started to lift her up into his arms.

"Daddy?" She said.

"Yes, honey, it's me. Let's go home." Greg whispered.

"What time is it?" Kara said as she rubbed her eyes.

"It's a little after 1 o'clock in the morning, just relax and I will carry you."

Kara sat up, as if she just realized she was awake and excited to be talking to her dad, "Daddy, I had so much fun today!"

"I heard; Jeff told me all about it," Greg said, still trying to whisper.

"Dad, I want to ride like Uncle Jeff," Kara said as she looked up at her dad.

"Let's talk about that later, sweetie," Greg said nicely, trying not to be dismissive about it.

"I'm serious Dad, I loved it almost as much as I love swimming. It was so much fun!" Kara was speaking like she wasn't tired at all anymore.

Realizing Kara was wide awake, Greg said, "Honey, Jeff and I talked about it and I am going to go riding with you guys sometime and we can talk about it more after that."

"Really? Do you know how to ride?" Kara asked innocently.

"Of course I do. Fishing is not the only thing I can do," Greg laughed, "but before we do that, we are going to go to Jeff's race next Saturday, up in Dallas. Does that sound fun?"

"Yes, I can't wait! Thank you, daddy!" Kara squeezed her Dad with a hug.

The next few days seemed to last forever to Kara. She was so excited! To her, it felt like waiting for Christmas morning, it seemed it would never come.

Greg had a good enough haul the first few days that he felt comfortable cutting his work week short by a day and was able to be home on Thursday night. He came in late in the evening, after Kara was already in bed. Like last week, he snuck into her room. He laid down on her little twin bed and gave her a big kiss on the cheek as he put his arm over her and whispered in her ear, "I love you honey. Do you want to go home or sleep here tonight?"

Greg knew that Kara felt like Jeff and Courtney's house was her home, since that was where she lived most of the year, but he always referred to his house as her home. To Kara, they were both home, and she felt love and peace at both houses.

"Hi, daddy," she said sleepily, rolling over to her side, so she was facing her dad. She briefly opened her eyes, smiled, and then closed them again. It was obvious to Greg that she was not fully awake or aware of the question he had asked. He was familiar with nights when he got home after she was in bed and most of the time she just stayed in bed. Greg would crash on Jeff's couch and they would go home in the morning. But Greg knew that she might want a better chance to make an aware decision tonight, due to the events planned for the next few days.

"Honey, do you want to go home? We have to leave for Dallas early in the morning, and I need to gather some things together to get ready." Greg was still whispering, but a little bit louder than he was before.

Kara opened her eyes suddenly and said, "Tomorrow is Dallas?"

"Yes, did you forget?" Greg asked with a smile.

Kara's eyes were now wide open and she leaned up in her bed, "No way dad, I can't wait. Let's go home." She then practically kicked Greg out of her bed so she could get out and head home. She was visibly excited and ready to go home.

She grabbed her bag and said, "I'm ready dad, I knew you were coming, and I'm ready to go to Dallas!"

"Well, we need to go home first honey. I'm glad you are so excited and ready to go. Let's go home and get some more rest then we will head out in the morning."

"Okay. What time do I need to wake up?" Kara asked happily.

"I don't know for sure, I will wake you up when I am packed and ready to go."

They headed to Greg's truck and started to drive home. After a few minutes, Greg noticed Kara in his rearview mirror as she sat in the middle of the backseat. She seemed very happy and began whistling one of her favorite tunes. Greg listened for a bit and then said, "Do you want to go out for breakfast tomorrow? We could go to Annie's and get your favorite pancakes."

Kara smiled and said, "Yes!" Then she went back to whistling.

The next morning, Greg was ready to go early, having had very little sleep, and they were on their way by regular breakfast time. After stopping to eat, the drive to Dallas was about six hours long. Greg was very happy to have the time to spend with Kara, but there are only so many things you can talk about with an eight year old, even when you're a fisherman who only sees his daughter a couple of days a week during most of the year. He was grateful to have a truck that had an overhead DVD player with a drop down screen, so Kara could entertain herself with some of her favorite movies and recorded television series.

She was just like any other kid on a road trip with parents… "How much longer is it?

And when Greg would tell her, she would ask a follow-up question, "Is that long, medium, or short? "

Greg thought to himself how much he loves spending time with Kara and he wished it were possible for him to spend every day with her, but he was very grateful to have a good brother and sister-in-law, who were willing and able to help him raise her with the values he believed in. It was also very important to him that his parents lived close enough to play a big role in her life as well.

After several more hours, a stop for lunch, a couple of stops to tinkle, and a short nap, they were nearing the big city of Dallas, Texas.

Greg softly said to Kara, "Sweetheart, look at what I see." He was looking in his mirror to see the reaction on her face, which was wide-eyed, very wide-eyed.

She stared out the front and side windows, the best she could, and grinned with a big smile and said, "Is that Dallas?"

"It sure is. That is Dallas," said Greg with confidence.

They were both silent for a few minutes, just looking at the big city getting bigger as they drove closer. After a while, Greg said, "Do you see that tall building with all the lights?"

"Yeah."

"Guess what that is."

"I don't know. What is a Daddy?" Kara asked, still having excitement in her voice.

"That is our hotel. That's where we are staying tonight and tomorrow night." Greg peaked in the mirror again, to see her reaction.

"It is? Honest?" Kara said joyfully.

"Yep, that is where we are staying this weekend. It's going to be fun. They have a pool, a movie theater, and even a bowling alley," Greg was acting as excited as young Kara was.

"In our hotel? Honest? Can we go bowling?" Kara asked, while kicking her feet up and down.

"I think we will have time for that. What good is a road trip without some swimming, bowling, and a good movie?" Greg stated, like it was a requirement.

"Are Jeff and Courtney staying there too?"

"Yes, they have a room nearby us and are probably already there. Do you see what is right over there, on the other side of the highway?" Greg was pointing at a large outdoor arena.

"What is it?" Kara asked

"What does it look like honey?" Greg asked his little girl, who had seen several smaller arenas.

"Is that where Jeff is going to race? It is so big!" Kara said as if it was certain.

"Cool, huh? That is what a big city track looks like."

"Wow," Kara was focused on the track, staring at it with those big sapphire eyes, "when can we go see it?"

"Jeff will take us over in the morning and we can watch him on some practice runs."

"I can't wait! This is going to be awesome! I love you daddy!" Kara said, both talking and singing.

"Love you, too, honey, I love you, too," he smiled as he pulled the truck into the hotel parking lot, "now let's go check out our room!"

Chapter 12 - Superman

The following morning, Kara was up before Greg, getting herself ready for the day. When Greg woke up and saw his girl all ready to go, he said, "Someone sure is excited to go to the track."

"When can we go?" Kara asked with eager anticipation.

"Let me get cleaned up quickly. I will call Jeff to find out what the plans are and then we can head down to the lounge for some breakfast," Greg said while he was washing his face.

"Awesome!" said Kara as she was dancing around the room.

Greg hurried as fast as he could to get ready, he did not want to make Kara wait. He had never seen her so excited about anything like this before, except swimming. When he was ready to go, he called his brother and did not get an answer so he called Courtney. "Hey, where is Jeff? He didn't answer his phone."

"He is already down at the track. He said QRM wanted him to test their new bike, so he wanted to get some runs in on his bike to get to know the track before doing that for them," Courtney had a noticeable irritation in her voice.

"You sound kinda mad. Is there something wrong with that?" Greg asked.

"I don't know. It just seems weird; I will tell you about it when we get there. Have you guys had breakfast?" Courtney asked, her tone sounding less upset.

"No, we were just about to go down. Have you?" replied Greg.

"No, not yet. I will be ready in five minutes. I'll meet you down there," suggested Courtney.

"We'll wait for you if you want," offered Greg.

"No way, that isn't necessary. Kara is probably hungry. Get her down and you guys start eating. I will just come down in a few," said Courtney.

"Cool. See you downstairs Sis," said Greg.

Greg then told Kara it was time to go eat and that they would then go over to the track with Courtney after eating because Jeff is already over there.

"Okay," Kara said simply.

On the way down to breakfast, Greg took an opportunity to show Kara one of his favorite things to do in fancy hotels. When they got in the elevator, he said, "Now I am going to show you something really cool to do on elevators."

"Really? Something cool to do on elevators?" Kara inquired.

"Yes. Now you watch the doors carefully, and when they are all the way closed, get ready to jump," Greg said as they were turning around in the elevator.

"To jump?" Kara said with a curious tone.

"Yes. When I tell you to jump, you jump as high as you can," said Greg with a half smile.

Kara was watching the doors intently as Greg pushed the button to take them down to the lobby. The doors closed and Kara looked at him, then a second later, he said, "Jump!"

They both jumped up into the air just as the elevator was starting its descent, so it made them feel like they had jumped extra high, and gave them a temporary feeling of weightlessness. When they touched back to the floor of the elevator, Kara was giggling and said, "That was fun daddy! It tickled my tummy! "

"Totally cool, huh?" Greg said, smiling.

Still giggling, Kara responded, "Can we do it again?"

"Every time we use the elevator girl! I love doing that! "Greg was matching Kara's enthusiasm for her simple, newfound form of fun. "Now get ready for the bottom. We can do it again at the bottom and it feels a bit different. Ready? Jump!"

Kara jumped as high as she could again, just as the elevator was coming to a stop at the lobby. Her jump was cut short by the momentum change, and she felt extra weight, or gravitational pull, nearly stumbling, as she hit the elevator floor. Kara giggled some more and was laughing as the elevator doors opened, and there were people waiting to get on.

A sixty something aged couple could see her happiness, and the woman asked, "Is this a fun elevator?"

People had a way of noticing Kara everywhere she went and always felt comfortable talking to her. Greg noticed this all the time and did not remember so many random people talking to him or Jeff when they were young and growing up, or any of their friends.

"We were jumping! You should try it!" Kara exclaimed.

This made the couple laugh, and the man said jovially, "Maybe we will."

Kara had expressed her excitement of the activities so enthusiastically to this couple that Greg could see the desk clerk look their way, having heard Kara exclaim their activities. He did not have a very pleasant look on his face. As they walked his way to go to the lounge, Kara said, "Good morning, nice man!" as they passed, and his demeanor quickly changed to a smile.

It was about 10 minutes later, as Greg and Kara were eating, that Courtney came to join them. They then all ate together, finished their food, and headed to the track. When they arrived and parked, Kara could hear the sounds of the motorcycles as she got out of the truck, and she started to run toward the stadium. Greg yelled mildly to her, "Kara, wait for us! Please don't run through the parking lot; it's dangerous."

Kara stopped and turned around, laughing, a pretend, slow laugh, and said, "Ha, ha, ha, I laugh in the face of danger!"

Greg turned to Courtney with a puzzled look on his face and simply said, "What the…?"

Courtney smiled and said, "That is from one of her favorite movies."

"Oh, yeah," Greg said, then addressing Kara, "Very funny honey, but a lion cub you are not. Now get over here and hold my hand before I track you down, pounce on you and tickle you to death!" They both laughed and walked together toward the stadium. Kara began singing a little song to herself.

Then Greg, when he saw the area was safe, said to Kara, "You can go and run ahead now; just stop up there by the gates until we catch up to you. You should be able to see the track from there."

"Woo hoo!" Kara exclaimed, as she took off towards the stadium in gates.

Courtney said, "Greg, you are such a good father."

Greg responded somberly, "Oh, thanks, but sometimes I don't feel like it. I have to be away so much. I sometimes wish I could somehow change professions so I did not have to miss so much of her life."

"Greg, you are a good father. No, a great father! The time you spend with Kara is always so meaningful, and you treat her like she is the most precious thing on earth. She loves you so much! She talks about you all the time and tells me every single thing she knows about you and all the things you tell her," Courtney said as she grabbed Greg's arm, just above the elbow.

Greg got a little tear in his eye as he responded, "She is the most precious thing on earth… I mean, since her Mom can't be with us. She is all I have, and I would do anything humanly possible to make sure she is safe, happy, and well cared for. I am so grateful to you and Jeff, and all that you do for her. I know I don't express it enough, but you both mean the world to me too. I could never leave Kara when I am out at sea, if I didn't know, with all my heart, that she was being cared for and loved the way I want her to be and the way her mom would be proud of if she were here."

Now Greg was crying more than just a tear as his emotions had overtaken him, which was very common when he talked about his precious little girl, and especially on the rare occasions when he would mention her mother.

Courtney had a tear in her eye now too; she grabbed Greg by the forearm with her other hand, so they stopped walking and they turned toward each other, "Thank you Greg; thank you for your kindness to us and thank you for trusting us with Kara. She brings us a lot of joy and helps to fill the void we have by not having our own kids. Sometimes I feel like that is part of God's plan; maybe even the reason we weren't able to have kids is so we were able to help raise Kara."

"I feel that way too, sometimes, but I would never presume to interfere with what you feel about not having kids. I just want you to know that I love you and Jeff and I am forever grateful for all you do for us," Greg was speaking slowly and meaningfully.

Courtney reached up and put her arms around Greg and they hugged and cried for a few moments together until Greg said, "Now let's get that little girl in to see your amazing husband!"

Greg and Courtney met Kara at the entrance to the stadium. Kara looked up at them, saw that they had both been crying, and reached for both their hands. She was a very perceptive child, and could feel the love the three of them had as a family.

When Kara grabbed their hands, both Greg and Courtney looked at each other immediately feeling a sense of peace and comfort. Kara had always had a way, with her simple touch, to instill peace and healing in the hearts and souls of others.

As the three of them entered the stadium, they could see a few riders going around the track, taking the bermed corners, and hitting the jumps, occasionally doing some sort of aerial tricks. They were still in the phase of warming up, so they were not going top speed, but Kara still exclaimed, "They are going so fast and jumping so high!"

"Where is Jeff?" She asked.

Courtney looked around for a few seconds, and said, "look for the one wearing all the Revved Up gear."

"Is that him, the one that just went off that jump over there?" Kara pointed to the opposite corner of the stadium.

"Yep, that's him. Good eye Kara," Courtney said as she squoze Kara's hand.

They stood at one end of the track for a few minutes and watched Jeff and the other riders run a few laps. Then they headed down to the crew area. Greg and Kara followed Courtney, as she was the one who had the access pass to get them all down where the action was.

There were riders, coaches, mechanics, reporters, sponsors, and all kinds of race support all over the place. Kara had never been to anything like this before. She had been to a few small circuit races that came through their small town area, and she had even been up to San Antonio one time to a big ice-skating show with Robert and Helen, but she had never been to something this big; something so big that it was going to be on television, not only in America, but also on television in other countries. Her eyes were so big and bright as she looked around at all the activity. She kept asking Courtney questions about who people were and what they were doing or what was going on in a certain area. She even asked if they could go stand behind one of the riders that appeared to be being interviewed by a television reporter.

Courtney said to her, "Jeff will definitely be interviewed by a reporter today and tomorrow, and I will tell him you want to stand by him during one of them."

"Really?" Kara asked with excitement, almost shouting with glee.

"Of course," Courtney responded with a smile, "he would love to have you! He always asks me to stand in with him, but I don't always like to. Sometimes TV people can be kind of rude. Sometimes the cameraman will intentionally zoom the camera so only Jeff is in the picture, so when it is shown on TV, all you can see is half my body or something."

Courtney realized what she was saying was sounding derogatory and probably not good to be telling Kara, who was so excited about the opportunity a minute ago, so she added, "But I am sure they would not do that to you. They like fresh new pieces of rider stories. I'm sure they would love to learn who you are and have Jeff say a few things about you."

"That would be totally awesome!" Kara then turned to Greg and asked, "Dad, is that okay?"

"Of course it is honey… But don't you go stealing the show from your uncle, okay?" he said with a grin.

Kara laughed a little, "Okay daddy, I won't. I promise."

Courtney turned to Greg and said, "I'm not so sure she will be able to help it. Jeff will probably really talk her up and you know what an unusual attraction she seems to have to people. They are just drawn to her everywhere we go."

Just then, they noticed that Jeff had stopped riding the track and turned off to head in the direction of the crew area. He looked around and found a small, clear space close to the three of them and spun the bike in a circle, kicking up a little dirt, stopped and repeated his sponsor's catchphrase, "That was totally awesome! Now all I need is a Revved Up!" He then slowly rode over to them.

"Nice entry, as always, honey," Courtney said sarcastically.

Jeff got off his bike, took off his helmet, walked over to them and gave Courtney a kiss and leaned down to Kara and said, "How is my little superstar rider today?"

Kara, who is not normally shy, especially around family, responded in a shy tone, "Good."

Jeff grabbed the handles of his bike and asked her, "Do you want to take it out for a spin?"

"Very funny, Jeff," said Greg, "don't mess with her head."

"Chill dude, she knows I'm just kidding around," Jeff reached over and punched Greg in the arm lightly.

Kara was just smiling.

"So how is the track?" Asked Greg.

"It's nice, man. It has some excellent berms and the final jump is perfect for aerials," Jeff said decisively.

Courtney interrupted, "Jeff, easy on the aerials. You know it is an unnecessary, added risk to do aerial tricks at a Supercross event. Save it for the freestyle aerial show tomorrow."

"I know honey. I will be careful and just do the tricks I have mastered. But you know how the fans are, they love the jumps. It is what they come to see, and the sponsors want us to do it too. It draws a crowd for them."

Just then, the QRM team came over to talk to Jeff. They pulled him aside for a few minutes and then he turned back to Greg, Kara, and Courtney and said, "I'm going to go ride the new QRM bike now. Hey Kara, do you want to see an awesome jump?"

"That would be totally awesome!" she said.

"Okay, you keep your eyes on me, and when I go over the final jump, right over there..." Jeff pointed to the start and finish line mound, "when you see me come to that jump, you just watch, I will do the superman for you."

Jeff then leaned over and gave Courtney a kiss and said, "I love you honey."

"I love you too, babe. Please be careful, you know how I feel about QRM. How do you even know the bike is safe?" Courtney said as she grabbed him by the forearm so he would know not to ride off quite yet.

"Court, don't worry, I know these guys. They are as meticulous as I am about their bikes, I am sure it is a great machine," he said as he pulled out the kickstarter.

Jeff gave her one more kiss, told Kara to keep her eyes peeled and headed over to the QRM team.

When Jeff was out of the area, Greg turned to Courtney and asked, "What were you going to tell me about QRM? You seemed to be nervous about something just now too."

"Well," Courtney paused, "the QRM guys have been bugging Jeff about riding for them for the past few years. Jeff has always been very nice to them, helping them with some ideas for their bikes, and testing some of them for them. They really spoil him sometimes and they have always helped us when things have been rough. They have been so good to work with, so Jeff feels like he should remain cooperative to them and help them, even though he does not want to leave Revved Up. QRM does not think Jeff is being reasonable. They have offered him so much more money than the Revved Up contract. It is all about money to them. I get a bad feeling about them. I don't feel like they have high morals, and would be willing to do anything to get him. Last time they met, he flat out told them that he would never ride for them and please stop asking. So I think it is odd that they still want him to test their new bike. I just have a bad feeling about it."

"I don't blame you," Greg said, "Sounds like kind of a sketchy deal to me too."

Kara had been watching Jeff getting ready to ride over at the QRM station while Courtney and Greg talked. Near the end of Courtney's explanation, Kara turned and was listening more intently. She could sense the nerves in Courtney and said to her, "I feel it too. Something bad is going to happen."

Courtney, knowing how perceptive Kara could be sometimes, ran over to Jeff and said, "Don't do it, Jeff, please don't ride for them. I don't have a good feeling about it."

Jeff, having not been part of the conversation with Greg and Kara, was focused on riding and helping out; what he considered to be "one of the members of the same big motocross family." He said to her, "It will be fine honey; everything is going to be fine. I will take just a few laps for them and be right back, just like I always am. I've done this thousands of times."

Courtney threw her arms around Jeff, squeezing him very tight, and said, "I love you. Dammit, I love you!"

Jeff responded, with somewhat of a puzzled tone, "I love you too; see you in a few minutes." He then gave the bike a kick to start it up, revved the engine a few times, and off he went to the track.

Courtney went back over to Greg and Kara, and the three of them watched as Jeff took off from the starting area, rounded the first corner, and headed through the first series of bumps. He twisted and turned through the track, just as easily as he normally would, but not quite as fast. The slower speed was typical for any rider the first time on a bike they were not familiar with. As he rounded the final corner and headed toward the finish jump, he began to accelerate. He appeared to be at or about his normal top speed when he hit the final jump. Kara's attention was fixed on Jeff like a deer in the headlights of an oncoming car. Greg and Courtney were also watching with close attention.

The superman aerial trick was one that Jeff had executed hundreds of times without any problems. The trick involves letting go of the handlebars and allowing the bike to go ahead of the rider while in the air. The rider then grabs the rear fender of the bike, with his body horizontal, gives it a tug toward him, and flies back to the handlebars to complete the trick as he lands.

Jeff hit the final jump, being propelled into the air with its force, and he began the superman trick. Just at that moment, it became very apparent to him, and everyone watching, that the trick was not going to end well...

The front wheel of the bike came off in mid air, leaving Jeff with just one wheel to land on. Having noticed this awful situation, Jeff hurried back to grab the handlebars and attempted to lean back on the bike before hitting the ground, hoping to be able to land on only the rear wheel and slow down enough to be able to safely crash off the back of the bike, which was something he was experienced and skilled enough to accomplish. However, another problem occurred. As he landed on the rear wheel, the tire burst, causing him to lose the balance he expected, and the front of the bike came forward abruptly, the front forks digging into the dirt like an anchor, which then caused the rear end of the bike to propel Jeff high into the air, like a trapeze artist.

Greg reached down to Kara to cover her eyes, not wanting her to see what was inevitably about to happen. Courtney let out a terrified scream as she dropped everything she was holding and started running out to the track as fast as she could, yelling and screaming as she ran.

"NOOOO!" She yelled, with a horrific screech, "NOOOO, NOOOO!"

Jeff, meanwhile, was flying through the air, out of control, about 15 feet high at peak, then headed toward the ground, headfirst, at an alarming pace. He was helpless. His body was at the mercy of the momentum the bike had given him, and he prepared himself, best he could, for impact, reaching his arms above his head in an attempt to soften the blow.

The next second was just that... only one second in time, but Jeff saw a glimpse of his life and what it meant to him. He did not know what would come after the impending impact, but he tried, best he could, to think of Courtney and how much he loved her. As he crashed to the ground, thinking about his life, he lost consciousness; his sight and mind when dark.

Chapter 13 - A Little Problem

Courtney was running and watching this all take place as Jeff hit the ground, landing with his head hitting the dirt first; his arms having a little effect protecting him from the collision with the hard packed landing area. The impact was felt by most of the small crowd who arrived early as they, practically in unison, let out an "ohh!"

The only thing anyone could do was watch him as his initial hit to the ground was followed by an uncontrolled roll, arms and legs flipping and flying, like a ragdoll, over and over again until he came to rest in a motionless heap.

When Courtney saw Jeff slam down to the ground, it sent a shock through her entire being. She could no longer run. She fell to the ground the moment he hit the same ground she was on, falling to her knees and pleading out to God that Jeff would be okay. She was crying and sobbing hysterically, rocking back-and-forth on her knees, right there on the dirt track. All the other riders had stopped by this time, seeing what had happened; some of them watching, and others running toward Jeff to help him.

Kara and Greg quickly ran to Courtney's side, kneeling down by her. Greg wrapped his arm around her, and Kara hugged her head. The three of them cried and prayed together while the track crews attended to Jeff, who was quickly surrounded by emergency workers.

"No, no, no!" Courtney began to repeat over and over again. "He just has to be okay. He is my life. He is everything to me. He just has to be okay!"

"The emergency staff will take good care of him," Greg said, doing his best to sound reassuring and confident.

Kara was crying with her.

"Help me over to him," Courtney pleaded to Greg, "I have to see him, I have to see him, I have to see if he's okay. Please help me get to him."

"Of course."

Greg helped Courtney up and the three of them walked carefully over to the scene of the accident. There were 10 to 15 emergency and track personnel already attending to Jeff and the emergency sirens could be heard as more help was on the way.

"Excuse me, please," Greg said to the workers as he tried to make his way, with Courtney and Kara, to Jeff's side. The crew all recognized Courtney and they let them proceed. She kneeled down next to him. He had been carefully turned onto his back. His helmet and all his gear were still on, with the exception of his goggles, which had snapped off in the fall.

Courtney leaned over Jeff so she could see into his eyes. They were closed. She was still crying terribly. As she looked at her man, he was crying, too, tears running down into his ears.

"Jeff?" She said quietly, trying to sound audible through her tears. "Jeff, can you hear me? Are you okay?" It seemed to her to be a silly question; he was obviously not okay, but she just needed to say something to him to see if he could respond.

The next 30 seconds lasted a lifetime. Then, while she was staring at his face, tears and snot running down hers, she saw his eyes open slowly and focus on her.

"Hi babe," he said to her surprisingly calmly.

Courtney smiled a half smile and sniffled through a little laugh, mixed with a sigh, showing obvious relief that Jeff was responsive.

"Hi," she said, "Are you okay?" It was still the only thing she could think of to say. She knew he wasn't, but she was so relieved that he was not dead or unresponsive that it was all she could muster up the strength to say.

"Courtney," Jeff began to say, "I have a little problem."

The way his voice sounded, and the way he was looking at her, Courtney knew that he had all his wits about him, "No kidding?" She said with a little burst of laughter. She was still crying, but trying to be brave and talk to him.

"Babe," Jeff said to her, quietly, but clearly, "I can't feel anything."

"What do you mean, you can't feel anything?" Courtney was fearing what she knew about accidents like this, that he may have broken his neck or back and suffered paralysis. The emergency personnel were also saying things to her about what he might mean and what his condition could be but she wasn't hearing them.

Jeff just looked at her for a moment, "I'm sorry, but I mean I don't feel anything. In my head I am trying to reach up and hug you, but nothing is happening with my arms. I can't feel anything at all."

Courtney's attempts to be brave for him just gave way to horror again and she burst into tears. "No Jeff, no," she said, "just don't talk right now. Your body is in shock or something."

Right at that moment, Jeff's eyes widened and said, "What is that?"

"What is what?" Courtney responded with a curiously confused tone and expression.

"I feel something now; I feel something on my ankle, what is it?" Jeff said, but could not look toward his feet.

Courtney turned to look at his feet, and she saw Kara with her hands resting on Jeff's ankle. She had her eyes closed and was very quiet and calm, like someone who was praying or meditating. Courtney just looked at her for a few seconds.

"What is it?" asked Jeff.

"It's Kara, she is touching your ankle. Do you feel it?" Courtney asked with some relief.

"I feel something on my ankle, but it does not feel like a touch," Jeff said slowly, as if he was struggling for words.

"What does it feel like?" asked Courtney.

"I don't know. It doesn't feel like anything. It feels like the sun or a warm light is shining directly through my ankle." he tried to explain.

Courtney then asked Kara, "What are you doing Kara?"

Kara turned and looked up at Courtney, like Courtney had never seen before. Kara's big blue eyes had that curious green tone and were bright as gems in a jewelry store and her smile was big and bright. Courtney felt like she was looking right into her soul, and they just gazed at each other until Kara said, "Jeff is going to be okay. He is hurt very badly, but he is going to be okay. His arms will hug you very soon."

Courtney listened to what Kara was saying; continuing to cry and struggling to smile at her sweet niece. They just gazed at one another some more, both of them smiling now, and crying at the same time. Courtney did not think anything of the moment, other than a sweet little girl; a very perceptive, sweet little girl, was trying to add comfort to a very difficult situation.

"Thank you, sweetheart," Courtney said to her, "that is very nice of you to say."

Kara removed her hands from Jeff and crawled on her knees to Courtney, and gave her a tender embrace, whispering in her ear, "He is going to be okay. I could see the two of you, hand in hand, walking together on the beach at sunset."

Courtney laughed another little laugh of relief and kindness through her tears and hugged Kara back, offering her another sincere, "Thank you Kara, you are very sweet."

At that moment, additional crew members arrived at the scene and told Courtney, Greg, and Kara that they needed to back away so they could attend to Jeff. They began carefully removing his helmet and cutting away some of his riding gear and clothes.

Courtney leaned over and gave Jeff a kiss on the lips, best she could to not get in the way, "I love you," she said.

"I love you too, babe," replied Jeff quietly, "I love you too!"

Chapter 14 - Time Will Tell

Courtney, Kara, and Greg held each other, crying, as they watched the emergency team position Jeff onto a stretcher board and carry him to the ambulance. As the doors shut, Courtney dropped to her knees again, then joined by Kara and Greg, and she released another vocal plea to the heavens, "God, I beg you, please take care of him! Please make him okay! He is my world, my everything. This is our life, his passion, our livelihood. I love him! I love you! I know you love him too, please take care of him."

Right then, Courtney felt a warmth at her side. It wasn't a feeling she'd ever felt before. It wasn't heat, it wasn't tingling, it was just a peaceful warmth. She turned her head and saw that the feeling was coming from where Kara was touching her. Then her mind caught a glimpse of Jeff, walking with her along the beach, hand in hand, just like Kara had said she'd seen. It was a beach she'd never been to or seen before. It was beautiful and Jeff was walking!

Kara looked up at her and said, "You can see it too?"

Courtney was taken back in thought and wonderment. "Could Kara see what she's seeing in her mind?" she thought to herself, "How could that be? She is a child."

Kara smiled and looked into Courtney's eyes and said, "Uncle Jeff is hurt very badly, but he's going to be okay. He will hug you, he will hold you, and he will walk with you again."

Courtney smiled a broken, tear filled smile, and said, "I don't know how or why, but I believe you are right. I saw it too. My Jeff is going to be okay. Thank you sweetheart."

They could no longer hear the ambulance, as the sirens had faded into the distance in the direction of the closest hospital, Dallas Regional.

"Let's go, I'll drive," Greg said.

The three of them gathered a few of their things and headed to Greg's truck. His diesel engine roared and he left parallel black marks in the parking lot as he spun the tires, taking off as fast as he could.

At the hospital, they had taken Jeff in through emergency and began running several tests. The first were a series of physical and visual assessments, then they performed a CT scan. When the results of the scan showed some vertebral damage, they gave Jeff an MRI to get a better look at the bones and tissues in his mid back.

"Where is he? Where is Jeff?" Courtney was pleading with the emergency department front desk nurses to direct her to wherever he was as she hurried into the hospital.

"Ma'am, I'll be happy to help you as soon as we verify who you are, and your relation to the patient," one of the nurses replied politely.

Courtney scrambled through her small bag for her identification and insurance cards. Her insurance card included her name and Jeff's name on them, listing her as his spouse. She presented those to the nurse who quickly gave her a thank you and made a copy.

"He's been taken up to surgery. You can take the stairs or the elevator to the second floor, hang right, and you will see the family waiting room. I will alert the team that you are there and they will send somebody out to speak with you as soon as possible," the nurse said kindly and slowly.

"Is he okay?" Courtney pleaded.

The nurse responded as calmly as she could, "I'm so sorry, but I do not have that information. Somebody from the neurosurgical team will speak to you as soon as they have news for you."

After what seemed to be a lifetime, but was only a couple of hours, a doctor came to the waiting room and approached the three of them.

"Are you Courtney?" he asked.

"Yes, doctor, I am. How is he? Is he okay?" Although Courtney had stopped crying for a while, just the sight of the doctor and anticipation of what he might say filled her eyes with tears once again.

"We did everything we could for Jeff. My son is a huge fan of his and I know he'd love to see him ride again. However, the reality is that he has a spinal cord injury. Jeff sustained an incomplete C7 fracture. We went in and placed some small, titanium support rods in the area which will give him the best chance of healing, but most of the time, with this type of injury, the patient does not fully recover."

The doctor paused.

"Meaning what, Dr.?" Courtney was listening very intently, but also very anxious to find out what she can expect in the coming days, weeks, months, and years. The thought of her husband not being able to do the things that he loves so much absolutely terrified her.

"I am so sorry to have to tell you this, but most individuals in cases like Jeff's never regain the ability to walk on their own power again," the doctor said with his hands clasped in front of him.

"Well, that's not gonna work out at all for us, doc," Greg said, "my brother will walk again. He is one of the strongest and most determined people I have ever known, he will walk again."

The doctor brought his hands up to his chest, still clasped, in sort of a praying gesture, "I appreciate your passion and desire for a full recovery. Time will tell. I just can't make any promises and can only speak from experience. I truly hope the best for him and for your family." The doctor extended his hand to Greg as he put his other hand on Courtney's shoulder "one of my team will be out in a few minutes to give you some more procedural information and go over some expectations for his stay here and recovery. Thank you and God bless."

A few minutes later, one of the nurses came out to speak to them, and explained that Jeff would soon be transferred to the intensive care unit for the next 7 to 10 days. He needed to be watched very carefully for neurogenic shock and other potentially serious complications like sepsis or other infections. She explained that once he is stabilized, he would be transferred to the rehabilitation wing for 1 to 2 weeks. At that point, depending on his progress, he would either be able to go home, or spend some more time in an offsite rehabilitation facility.

"Can we see him?" Courtney asked.

"When he is transferred over to ICU, we will give you the room number and security code so you may go visit him. The nurses on that wing will explain the visiting procedures and restrictions." She began to walk away, but then turned and reached out to embrace Courtney and as she did, she spoke softly in her ear, "this is going to be a difficult and trying journey for you and your family. I wish you nothing but the best!"

As the nurse left, Greg said to Courtney and Kara, "now that we have some news, let's go down to the cafeteria and get something to eat. Then we will go see him in the ICU. Sound good?"

Courtney smiled and nodded and Kara said, "Yes daddy."

For most of the next year, Jeff and Courtney spent their time going back-and-forth to medical appointments and physical therapy. In the early weeks, Courtney had to do almost everything for Jeff, as he had lost most of the use of his arms, and all of the use of his legs; but as time progressed, so did Jeff. After about six months, he was able to get himself around on his own, using his arms for mobility and a wheelchair to get around the house, to stores, therapy, and do a little work in his motorcycle shop.

Chapter 15 - Scrap Metal

Another several months went by and Jeff and Courtney had settled into their new routines of life with a wheelchair and limited abilities. Kara was very accepting of it and even thought it was cool, especially when Jeff would tilt his chair back and without much effort at all, just balance in a wheelie. Sometimes he would spin around and try to do little tricks, like rocking up on the right or left wheel for a few seconds, he called it his "two wheeled unicycle with a twist."

One afternoon, exactly one year after Jeff's accident, he approached Courtney while she was in the kitchen making something for the two of them to eat for lunch.

"Hi beautiful, what are you doing?" Jeff asked.

"The usual, I'm just making us a little lunch," Courtney responded without turning around.

"How about you stop doing that and we go out for lunch to celebrate?" Jeff said with more fervor in his voice.

"Celebrate what?" she asked skeptically, "what is there to celebrate, Jeff?"

"It's been one year since my accident," he said with a smile, but Courtney hadn't turned around yet.

"I know, Jeff, I have been thinking about that lately. I have been thinking about how much you want to walk and how hard you've been working with your therapies, but nothing seems to be changing." Courtney began to cry, "I know it's been a year now, but it doesn't feel right to celebrate."

Jeff moved toward Courtney until he was right behind her. He grabbed her by the waist and pulled her down onto his lap, wrapping his arms around her tightly as he spoke directly into her ear, "I want to show you something. Please come to lunch with me to celebrate, and you will understand."

Courtney's tears were starting to diminish as she said, "show me what, baby?"

"Come to lunch with me and I will show you something amazing.."

"It's not another wheelchair trick, is it?" Courtney interrupted, with a slight laugh in her voice.

"Ha, ha, no. Come to lunch with me and I will show you," Jeff matched her little laughter.

"Okay, okay, where are we going?" Courtney asked, as she leaned back into his chest.

"Don't worry about it, I have something planned," Jeff's voice had turned noticeably more excited now. "You go get ready and I will get the truck and meet you outside."

About fifteen minutes later, Courtney came out of the house through the garage and saw Jeff sitting in his wheelchair in the garage with the truck parked out on the street.

"What's going on?" She asked.

Jeff gave her a hand motion in his direction and said, "Come here, babe, I want to show you something." As he said this, he gave his wheelchair a backwards roll and rolled to the edge of the garage area at the beginning of the driveway, still facing Courtney, watching her carefully as she walked slowly toward him.

When she got just a few feet from him, he reached behind him and pulled out a long piece of metal and rubber that resembled some sort of motorcycle part, or maybe a few parts of a bike put together into a shaft of some sort about 3 feet long.

"Uh, what is that?" Courtney asked in a playful tone.

"Well, it's a homemade cane," Jeff said proudly.

"A cane?" Courtney asked sarcastically, "that hunk of metal is a cane?"

"Ya, do you like it? I made it myself, back in the shop," Jeff was excited to show Courtney the cane he had made, but she was much less excited, as evidenced by the dismayed look on her face.

"We are going out to lunch to celebrate that you made a cane? One thing for sure, you can tell it's homemade," she laughed a sarcastic laugh.

"Very funny. Of course not silly! I lost the use of my legs, not the use of my brain, remember?" Jeff was matching her tone.

They both laughed a second or two, as Jeff set the makeshift cane to the side of his chair and said, "now you just stand right there and watch what I've been working on," Jeff paused as he brought his hands to the armrest of his chair with his elbows pointing up, as if he was going to get out of the chair, like the way he would if he was transferring to bed or to a couch or recliner, "and about the surprise… no, I am not talking about this awesome cane, which I like very much and I'm very proud of by the way." Jeff winked and smiled.

Courtney stood there and watched, as the love of her life bowed his head down and pushed himself up from the wheelchair, slowly and carefully, until he was standing in front of it, looking directly at her with a huge smile on his face. She matched his smile and began to get a tear in her eye when Jeff said, "Wait, that is not all."

He reached to the side of his chair, grabbed the cane he had made, and brought it to his right side, locking his right elbow with his arm straight. What he did next, Courtney was unsure if she'd ever see again in her life. Jeff took a slow, limping step toward her, then, using a rocking momentum, took another step using the cane for support. He was right in front of her, they were both smiling ear to ear, Courtney crying, as Jeff said, "May I walk you to the truck, my love?"

She had a small burst of joyful laughter through her tears and said, "Of course you can, baby, of course you can!"

Jeff extended his arm for Courtney to hold onto, which was something he was both doing to be a gentleman, as well as to use her for some extra support with his new efforts to walk. As he extended his arm, he turned toward the truck, and then began to take one, slow, unsteady step at a time, down the rest of the driveway toward the truck. The process took several minutes, but Courtney loved every second of it, and was filled with emotion for the success her husband had made in his therapy efforts.

"Jeff, how long have you been walking?" She asked.

Jeff paused for a moment and replied, "I took some steps a couple weeks ago, at rehab, while holding onto the parallel bars on both sides of me. The therapist said I wasn't ready..." Jeff turned his head toward Courtney with a mischievous grin, "he shouldn't have doubted me, and he shouldn't have left me alone for a couple minutes."

They both laughed and Courtney said with a little song in her voice, "That's true. Never doubt my man."

"Then when he returned," Jeff continued, "and I was in the bars myself, I convinced him to help me give it a go, and I came home that afternoon, went out to the shop and built this totally awesome cane."

"It looks like the handlebars to a bike. Isn't that a little ironic?" Courtney said.

"That's the point," Jeff responded, with a resounding surety, as they got to the truck and he rested up against the passenger side, placing the makeshift cane up against the rear door, "these are actually the handlebars from the crappy QRM bike that did me in last year. I dismantled the entire bike and I wanted to make things out of it that would remind me to never take anything for granted. I always want to be reminded of the day my life took a dramatic change, and I look forward to the day that I will take this cane and throw it down, never to need it again!"

Courtney could see Jeff's pain and passion all over his face. She leaned her body up against his, sliding both her hands down his forearms until she was holding both his hands. She stood up on her toes, so she could speak softly and directly in his ear, and said, "Jeff, I love you so much! I am so proud of how hard you have been working and the effort you have been putting into getting better. I love you! I love you! I love you!"

She then kissed him passionately. They kissed and held each other tightly, leaning up against that truck, parked at the side of the road, for the next few minutes, like young, passionate teenage kids, who were kissing for the first time.

On the way to one of the local restaurants to have lunch, they did not talk very much. Both of them were enjoying the moment they had just experienced together. Jeff would turn his eyes from the road for a few seconds to look at Courtney and she would be looking at him smiling. He was still using the adaptive hand controls to operate the truck, but they both knew that it was only a matter of time before those could be removed.

At lunch, Jeff had something else very important to share with Courtney. He started, "Babe, you know how we have talked in the past about what I should do when I retire from racing?"

"Yeah, we've talked about a few things; motorcycle design and sales, custom bikes, racing team training. What are you referring to?" Courtney asked before taking a bite of her salad.

"You're right. We have talked about a number of things and I think you know that I have never really felt comfortable with any of those, mainly because when we have talked about it, retirement was still a ways off, so we have not really felt like we needed to be solid on something," Jeff explained.

"That's true," Courtney felt a sudden sorrow for not having given it much thought over the past year. "Honey," she said, "I'm sorry I haven't talked to you about what comes next if you wanted. I just never wanted you to feel pressured on making a decision when you were focusing on getting better."

"No, that is not what I'm getting at Court," Jeff was not angry at all, "I understand you feeling that way. I did too. Please don't worry about that."

Courtney smiled, "What then?"

"Well, part of the reason I don't feel concerned about the fact that we never really talked about it is kind of what you said, I was getting better. Although I had every amount of will and determination to get on my feet again, I just did not know for sure if I would ever be able to," Jeff was speaking somberly.

"I did, I always believed in you. I knew you would," Courtney said softly, almost so softly that Jeff did not hear. It was almost like she was keeping something to herself.

"What?" Jeff asked as he could tell something else was on her mind, "What is it?"

There was a pause before Courtney said again, "I did, I knew it," she said it louder this time, so she knew Jeff could hear her.

"Babe, I love that you have such great confidence and belief in me, thank you!"

"That's not what I'm saying, Jeff," Courtney looked straight into his eyes as she continued, "Yes, I do have every confidence and faith in your determination, but what I am saying is that I knew you would walk again."

"You did? What do you mean? How could you know?" Jeff appreciated her believing in him, but had a slight frustration in his voice because he did not understand what she meant.

Courtney paused for a few seconds more and said, "Do you remember the day of the accident? I mean, I know you remember the day, but how much do you remember of the immediate few minutes after the accident?"

Jeff thought for a moment, "I remember everything being dark and hearing your voice, like it was calling me from another room in a dark house. When I was able to consciously open my eyes, the first thing I saw was your beautiful face."

Courtney smiled.

"What is it that you are asking me?" Jeff's curiosity peaked.

"Do you remember when you felt Kara touching your ankle?" She asked hesitantly.

"Yes, of course I do. It was like nothing I've ever felt before," he replied.

"Could you hear her? Do you remember what she said?" Courtney asked slowly.

"No, honey, I couldn't hear her. The only thing I remember is you telling me that it was Kara who I was feeling touching my ankle; but I remember it did not feel like a touch. It felt more like a bright light or sun shining on that spot of my body. In fact, it felt like the sun was shining right through my body," Jeff hadn't talked about this feeling much since the day of the accident and he spoke passionately about it.

"Yes, I remember you describing it that way," Courtney confirmed.

"So what about it Courtney? What does that have to do with me walking?" Jeff asked kindly.

"Maybe nothing," she paused, trying to gather the thought she wanted to express. In her mind, she knew exactly what she wanted to say. She wanted to tell Jeff that she thinks Kara somehow knew he would walk again, but she knew Jeff would not understand if she just blurted that out. So she took a few moments and thought about her words.

"What then?" Jeff asked with increased curiosity, almost starting to laugh because of the way Courtney seemed to be shying away from talking about something that didn't make sense to him at the moment.

"Well," Courtney started slowly, "when Kara was touching your ankle that day, she told me that you were going to be okay."

Jeff smiled, "Of course she did. You know what a sweet girl she is, and how perceptive she is to the feelings of those around her."

"No, I know," Courtney was still having trouble expressing exactly what she wanted to tell Jeff, "no, that's not it at all." She continued, "Kara told me that you were going to be okay, but then she said something else," a tear began to form in the corner of Courtney's eye and slowly rolled down her face.

Jeff reached across the table and gently took her hand, "What sweetheart, what else is there?"

"When Kara said you were going to be okay, my initial reaction was the same. I thought nearly the same thing you were saying right now, that she is just a sweet kid and perceptive of people's feelings," Courtney looked at Jeff right in his eyes to make sure she had his full attention, which she did, "I was so worried about you and focused on how you were doing, but then, when she let go of you she came toward me and hugged me to tell me something else."

Courtney was crying more now and Jeff took her hands with both of his, "Go on babe, what else is there?"

"Kara hugged me and told me again that you were going to be okay, that your arms would soon hug me, and that she could see us walking together," tears were streaming down Courtney's face now, and she was smiling through her tears as she went on, "and when she told me this, I felt what you described your ankle felt when she touched you. I felt a warmth like nothing I had ever felt before. I felt like the sun had turned its focus just to me, and at that moment, what I was hearing that little girl tell me just felt right, like I knew it was going to happen."

Jeff listened as Courtney was expressing these sensitive feelings and was thinking back to the day of the accident, trying to see the scene in his head of Courtney and Kara sharing this experience together as he lay motionless on the ground. Although he remembered the trauma, what she was saying felt good to him. He knew his wife was telling him something very important, and very true. He began to get teary eyed too.

Courtney said, "Does that make any sense at all?" She needed to feel like Jeff understood, even though she was not sure she even did. She needed to feel like he was connecting with her, validating what she was feeling.

"It's hard to understand," Jeff said, "if there is even anything to understand. I mean, it sounds like you felt similar feelings to what I experienced, but in greater effect, when Kara hugged you."

"I have gone over it in my mind so many times," Courtney started to talk a little faster now, the tears having subsided, "I have tried to rationalize what I felt as the emotions of the moment, but whenever I do, I can't help but think how real the feeling was. It was so reassuring, so strong, it almost seemed to be a feeling with tangibility." She leaned a little closer to Jeff, "So I stopped trying to make sense of it, and just accepted it as marvelous, maybe even miraculous foreshadowing of our life. What Kara saw, I do not know. What she was trying to tell me, if anything, I do not know. But what I do know is how I felt, and that can never be taken away from me, and I have stopped trying to play it off as nothing. It was real, it happened, and today we walked together down our driveway to the truck. It is not something I ever pictured, but when Kara told me she saw us walking together, I knew it was true and felt I could see it too." Courtney's tears had returned, and Jeff could feel the intense emotion of what she was saying and feeling when she continued, "I knew it was true. I knew you would walk again!"

Jeff leaned toward her and kissed her lightly on the lips, "I love you, Courtney, I truly love you. Thank you for being by my side through all of this. Thank you for believing in me."

Chapter 16 - Remix Racing Academy

After Jeff and Courtney had received and began eating the rest of their lunch, Courtney was thinking about the conversation they had about her experience the day of the accident, and how she felt about it, and it occurred to her that it was not what Jeff started out talking about. She took a break from her meal and said, "Jeff, I'm sorry. I just realized that you started talking about what you wanted to do going forward, and I totally took the conversation into something else."

"It's okay, I am glad we talked about that day and were able to share our mutual experiences again, as well as our individual feelings and experiences of the day. I can't believe you have never told me that before," Jeff expressed with care.

"I know. I just didn't want you to feel like I was trying to put pressure on you to get better or anything," Courtney reiterated.

"I understand, sweetheart, it's not a problem," Jeff said, as he took a bite of his food.

"So what did you want to tell me?" Courtney asked.

Jeff smiled, held up a finger as he finished chewing, and said, "I'm just going to come right out and say it… I want to train young riders to race."

"Really?" Courtney was a bit surprised, that was never one of the options they had discussed.

"Yeah," Jeff said excitedly, "I think it would be awesome, they have so much passion for the sport!"

"When did you come up with that idea?" Courtney inquired.

"Actually, it was just a couple weeks before my accident," Jeff took another bite of food and chewed before he continued, "do you remember the time I took Kara out riding with me?"

"Of course I do, you were so excited when you came home; so amazed at how well Kara could ride as a first time rider," Courtney was paying close attention while eating at the same time.

"Well," Jeff looked into Courtney's eyes with a focused intent, "I loved that feeling! I loved being able to share in the joy of a young rider the first time on their bike, learning to tear around the trails and tracks, learning to handle the power of the engine and maneuverability of the controls." Jeff chuckled, "I love helping others find the excitement that has brought me so much fun and success in my life!"

"Wait Jeff," Courtney interrupted, "you know that most kids would not learn as quickly as Kara. You said it yourself: you couldn't believe how well she rode, "like she's been riding her whole life," you said. The other kids are not all going to be like that, in fact, maybe no other kid will be able to ride that easy the first time."

"I know. I have considered that. I know there is going to be a lot of patience required. I have thought about that more than once, but I think I can handle it. In fact, I know I can handle it," Jeff said confidently.

They both thought for a few minutes as they finished most of their food. Courtney, thinking of the stress this may cause Jeff if it doesn't go the way he plans and Jeff thinking about what he could say to help Courtney understand that he is totally serious about opening a motocross training facility.

"Court, honey, I know this is taking you by surprise, and that is not what I really meant to do. I just wanted to show you today that I am ready to move on with our lives, to take the next steps, pun intended, together for our future," Jeff said as they both smiled.

"What are you going to call your program? Do you know yet?" Although Courtney was indeed surprised by this new information, she was trying to be supportive and ask in an upbeat way, rather than doubting and sarcastic.

"I don't know yet. I was hoping you would be able to help me with that. You are always so creative," suggested Jeff.

Courtney put her fork down on her plate and slid it slightly to the middle of their table, signifying she was done eating, and said, "Okay then; I don't hate the idea and I know you would be the best trainer in the country. How about we take the weekend to talk about it some more, and if we both feel good about it, great, let's do it."

Jeff pushed himself up from the table as quick as he could, balancing himself on the corner, as he leaned forward and kissed Courtney happily and excitedly. "Yes!" He said, "I love you, honey!"

Jeff and Courtney did just that; they spent the weekend talking about the idea of opening a training facility and what expenses, time, resources, advertising, and funding it would require. They had received a sizable payout from QRM after the accident, and could use that to start the business, but the biggest decision was if it was the right thing to do or not?

When Sunday evening came, they were sitting in the family room. Kara had just arrived to spend the week with them while Greg went out to sea for the week. Courtney sat up from laying her head on Jeff's lap and said, "I've got it!"

"You've got what?" Kara asked, but was not answered directly.

"I know the name of the training facility!" Courtney said excitedly.

"Cool," Jeff said, "I knew you would come up with something, what is it?"

Courtney turned to Kara and told her briefly about their plans they had discussed over the weekend.

Kara grinned as big as could be, then Courtney said, "Kara, how would you like to be the first student ever trained by the great Jeff Landers at the," Courtney paused and said, "wait for it," she paused some more, and then said with glee, "the Remix Racing Academy!"

"Awesome!" Kara shouted.

Jeff repeated quietly to himself, "Remix Racing Academy... Remix Racing Academy, hmm." Then he said to Courtney, "I love it! Does this mean you feel good about it?"

"I do honey. I do," Courtney wrapped her arms around Jeff and continued, "I think we should do it. It's going to be the greatest motocross training facility in the country! Because you are going to be the best coach in the country!"

"Oooohooo baby!" Jeff hollered, "Let's do it!"

"Now we just have to get my dad to let me," Kara said, with some noted doubt in her voice.

"True dat," Jeff said to her, "but I think all we need to do is get him out riding with us so he can see how awesome you already are and he will understand why you want to ride."

"Do you really think so?" Kara pleaded

"Darn right I do, little girl! Once he sees that you can whip his butt on a motorcycle, he will be like 'Holy crap, I got to get this kid on her own bike!'" They all laughed together.

"I hope you are right, uncle Jeff," Kara said as she pulled her legs up to her chest and hugged them, rocking back and forth with excitement.

The following weekend, Greg was able to go riding with Jeff and Kara. After seeing his daughter ride for just a few minutes, he turned to Jeff and said, "Holy shit bro, I thought you were exaggerating her ability to ride. Why am I not surprised that she is just as awesome as you said? Let's do this. Let's get Kara riding her own bike and start training with you!"

Chapter 17 - Opening Day

The next several months were spent getting some nearby land acquired, excavating the riding areas, building a small shop, garage, and classroom building, and doing a lot of advertising for Remix Racing Academy. The plan was to open June 10th, the first Monday after most traditional schools across the country would be ending for summer.

Jeff had been training Kara during the construction and development of the facility and had asked her to be his demonstrator on opening day, to show all the prospective students and their families how well she could ride after being instructed by Jeff, even though she was only 10 years old. Courtney had purchased her new riding gear, with graphics, that they all loved, and Greg even bought her her very own bike, one that was the proper size and power for her age and abilities. All of her equipment and gear were decorated in the Remix Racing Academy logos and colors. She was very proud and happy to represent Jeff and his new company.

Greg, of course, was there on opening day. He wouldn't have missed it for anything. It was all Kara would talk about when they were together, even when she was swimming; she would dry off and talk about riding. He knew that she had found a new passion, and was proud to be supportive of her.

He was at the new track a couple hours before the grand opening, watching Kara take some warm-up runs. He was thinking to himself how great she was at riding, and how proud he was of her and how happy he was for her to be able to show her skills to everyone that day.

Kara, after a few laps, saw her dad standing over by the small pit area and rode over to him, stopped, and turned off her bike and gave him a big hug. "I am so happy you are here daddy!"

"Are you kidding? I wouldn't miss this for anything!" Greg said back to her excitedly.

"But you had to miss some days of work," Kara was genuinely concerned about that.

"I know. It's okay. Like I said, I wouldn't miss this for anything. I can't wait to see you show your stuff to all the people today," Greg gave her a little wink. "Are you nervous?"

"A little," Kara said as she shrugged her shoulders.

"Well, you are going to do great! I just know you are!" Greg smiled and gave her another hug, "but you know, as your father, I have to tell you to make sure you are careful. Don't get carried away, just focus on what Jeff has trained you on and stick to it. Okay?"

"I will daddy. I love you!" She then stood up on her feet, with her motorcycle between her legs, "I have to get back to practice now." She gave the starter a kick and she went back to the track.

Greg went and found Jeff and asked, "Hey man, is there anything I can help you with?"

"Will you run the concession stand?" Jeff, who was busily working on some of the bikes for the visitors to try out on the track, responded without even looking at Greg.

"Really, you don't have anybody for that?" Greg paused, Jeff still hadn't looked at him, "I guess I could, if that's what you need."

"Just kidding bro," Jeff laughed as he looked up at Greg smiling, "I'm messing with you. I just wanted to see what you would say. I have a couple girls hired to run that for me today."

"Very funny dude," Greg lightly hit Jeff in the arm with his fist, something that they did from time to time since they were boys when they were goofing around with each other. "Seriously, I am here to help. What do you need?" he reiterated.

"That's awesome," Jeff said, "would you mind helping Courtney with hanging the final marketing signage that just came yesterday?"

"No problem," Greg turned to walk away, but then stopped and turned back and put his hand on Jeff's shoulder, "Hey, Jeff, I want to tell you how proud I am of how hard you have worked to make this day happen. I know we don't talk all that much, but I want you to know that I recognize how difficult this must have been for you."

"Thanks Greg," Jeff said, as he hit Greg on the shoulder in return.

"No really," Greg continued, "I really think it is awesome that you never gave up. You worked and worked and worked until you could literally get back on your feet and start something new. It's very impressive. I remember saying to the doctor, in the hospital, the day of your wreck that you would walk again. There's just no stopping you, man!"

"Thanks again," Jeff stopped working on one of the demo bikes he was doing some final tuning on, sensing he should give Greg more attention as he continued.

"I want you to know that I love you and Courtney and appreciate what you have done for Kara. You have put a lot of trust in her today. I appreciate that you are doing everything you can to make her happy and successful, it means the world to me. Thank you!" Greg gave Jeff a light hug.

"That is one special girl you have there, Greg," Jeff said, "I can't believe how fast she learns things, and how well she perceives things. It is truly amazing! It is our pleasure to help you out with her; she brings a lot of joy into our home."

"Thank you, thank you." They gave each other a thumb/wrist rap handshake and pulled each other into another quick hug, and Greg said, "Good luck today. I'm going to go find Courtney now. See you out there."

Jeff went back to working on the bikes and Greg went to help Courtney as he said he would. It was only an hour until opening and people had begun parking out in the nearby fields, which had been cleared for that purpose. Greg observed this and said to Courtney, "It looks like we have some early birds, that's a good indication of a successful day."

"I hope you're right, Greg," she said to him nervously. "Jeff has been working so hard on this, and is so wrapped up in it being successful. It would be so detrimental if it failed."

"It's not going to fail," Greg said enthusiastically, "this place is awesome! Have you seen how many social media followers RRA already has? You haven't even opened yet."

"That's true," Courtney said, following a sigh, "I guess that is a good sign, as well as the people that decided to get here an hour early." They were both working on hanging a sign for one of their sponsors on the inside of the track wall, "Hey, look at that family... They look like they are going to win the prize for biggest motorhome today." Courtney was pointing to a family who was just getting out of their motorhome. It looked like a rockstar tour bus and was pulling an equally impressive trailer.

Greg looked over to the field, "Holy crap, you are right. That thing is huge. And what is with the massive trailer, it looks like they are planning to move in or something."

They laughed, and Courtney said, "Some of the motocross fans get so into it. It becomes their life. I guess that is good for Jeff and I as we start this new venture."

"Are you trying to be as ironic as possible Courtney?" Greg said sarcastically.

"Totally," she said, "I know what you mean, Jeff and I are exactly the same way. This sport is who we are. It is who we have been and most likely always will be. Which is why this day is so stinking important that it just has to be successful. This could make or break us."

"It's going to be great," Greg said, "don't worry, it is going to be great!"

They finished putting up the signage and went to have a last-minute talk with Jeff and the rest of his employees and volunteer support crew. There was a lot of excitement in the room, and Jeff was so noticeably excited that it looked like he was going to throw down his cane and start doing jumping jacks or cartwheels or something.

Once everybody had gathered together and settled down, Jeff asked Greg if he would offer a few words of encouragement to everyone. Greg agreed and offered thanks to God and asked for blessings of safety and success in prayer as well. Then just spoke to them for a few minutes about what would make today successful and had them all gather close together for a cheer, "RRA, RRA," they began to chant at Jeff's direction, "Goooo Remix!" They all shouted together, excited to get to the front gates and get the day started.

Jeff made his way to the front of the small group, which now included some local dignitaries, including the mayor of their small town. They greeted each other, and Jeff looked out at the crowd, waiting to come in, "Wow," he said, "are you all in the right place?" There was a small roar of laughter through the crowd along with a lot of cheering.

"I'm not going to stand here and bore you with some speech today," Jeff began addressing the crowd formally, "I don't imagine any of you came today to hear my yapper do some yappity yappin... So I just want to thank you all for coming to the official grand opening of the Remix Racing Academy. I hope you enjoy it as much as I envision you will," he then took the obnoxiously large pair of scissors, which, like his cane, he made from parts of the old QRM bike and shouted, as he cut the ribbon provided by their major sponsor, Revved Up energy drinks, "let's get this totally awesome party started!"

Chapter 18 - An Unexpected Danger

There was a lot going on that day at the opening of RRA: from concessions and paraphernalia sales, to brief explanations from Jeff, as to what the students would be getting who trained with him; there were tours of the shop and track areas and, of course, there were bikes to demo and what Jeff called his "prized jewel of opening day" to be taking place at exactly noon.

Jeff's "prized jewel" was how he referred to Kara's demonstrative ride she was going to make for the crowd. Up to that point, she had spent most of the morning meeting with visitors, and showing off the gear which bore the names of both RRA and their other sponsors. She was very popular with the girls who decided to come visit, but at ten years old, the boys her age weren't interested in seeing a girl ride and the older boys were "too cool" to care. Kara thought the attention from the girls and their parents was cool and just laughed at the way some of the boys were acting.

Then the time came for her ride. It was straight up 12 o'clock and Courtney had made an announcement 10 minutes earlier that the main event would be starting at the track very shortly. Kara's nerves were racing like her dirt bikes cylinders at high RPM's now and Greg had come to talk to her and reassure her that she was going to be great, as Jeff was giving her some last-minute pointers and reminders to execute while she was riding. The plan was for her to be announced, make five circuits around the course, including one jump at the end of each circuit. The jumps were not to be anything fancy, just a basic jump to show the control she had with the bike.

Jeff quieted the crowd over the PA system. He announced who she was and what she was going to do and off she went, racing toward the first curve, then back and forth toward the second corner, through the berms and bumps, just like she had practiced, executing as close to perfect as was possible in motocross racing. Then it came time for the final jump and she did not follow the directions Jeff had given her. She increased her speed much faster than she needed to as she approached the finish hill. Greg grabbed Jeff by the arm and said, "Is she supposed to be speeding up like that?"

Jeff did not respond. They were both watching as there was no time to do anything else, just watch. Kara reached the final jump, which propelled her into the air, much higher than she had ever practiced. As she did, she gave her bike a nudge forward and let go of the handlebars, letting herself float back to the back of the bike. She kicked her legs out behind her as she grabbed the back of her seat and pulled the bike back towards her and flew into her original positions with her hands, feet, and butt where they belonged before landing on the bottom section of the landing area. She had just executed, perfectly, her first Superman aerial trick.

The crowd erupted with cheers and Jeff reached back at Greg with both arms, grabbing him by the shoulders, without looking at him, and exclaimed, "Holy shit, Greg, your ten year old daughter just did a fifty foot Superman in front of thousands of people! I've never taught her that."

Jeff, Greg, and Courtney ran out to the track, up to the finish area as Kara slowed the bike, spun it around a couple of times, and rode back up to where they were standing to meet her. They had been joined with some of Jeff's track and sponsor volunteers and crew, and they were all cheering and giving each other high-fives in celebration of the excellent demonstration Kara just put on. Jeff took a microphone from one of the crew and shouted to the crowd, "Ten year old Kara Landers, everyone!" The crowd shouted and cheered as Jeff continued, "Wasn't that amazing?" Then he let out a "woo hoo! I love this sport!"

Meanwhile, Greg was with Kara, who had taken off her helmet, and he said, "What were you thinking out there? You gave us all a heart attack, making a jump like that." Greg was definitely concerned, but also did not want to take away from his daughter's moment, "have you ever done that before?"

"No dad," Kara said, still shaking with excitement and an exhilaration of adrenaline, "no, I haven't, but when I came around the last corner, I could see myself doing it as some sort of tribute to Jeff and I knew I would be okay, so I just went for it."

"You just went for it all right," Greg said, "that scared the living crap out of me, but was also totally, totally awesome. I'm glad you are okay."

Jeff went right to answering questions from the fans and prospective students that came to the opening, he was inundated with questions about the safety of the program, and if it was realistic to expect other 10-year-olds to ride like Kara. As he answered all the questions, best he could, he took notice of a family standing at the back of the crowd. It was just a man with what looked like his wife, a daughter, and a son. The son looked to be about 10 or 11 years old. They were all just standing, with their arms either folded or in their pockets. Just watching the crowd and observing the questioning and answering. Jeff thought their demeanor seemed a bit odd, but didn't think too much of it as he was otherwise occupied.

After about an hour of questions, answers, and even some autograph signing, the crowd started to thin out. Jeff had received some serious inquiries to the program and signed up a handful of students from around Southern Texas, who would begin training with him for the summer the following week. He had turned his back on the small crowd to put some of his paperwork down for just a few seconds. When he turned around again, he found that the peculiar family he had noticed, watching from the back earlier, had walked up to him and were all standing within a few feet of him. Jeff offered a friendly, "Hello, thank you for coming today. What questions can I help you with?"

"Hi Jeff," the father of the family extended his hand toward Jeff and continued, "my name is Brady Stewart, and this is my wife, Candice, and our daughter Annie." He made no mention at that time of the boy who was with them. "We have been fans of yours for quite some time."

"Thank you," Jeff said sincerely.

"We were very sad about your accident and wanted you to know that our thoughts and prayers were with you. We are very glad to see you doing so well," Brady said.

"Thank you, that means a lot to me. I appreciate all the fan support I received during that time." Jeff looked down at the young boy in the family, who was still folding his arms, with a serious look on his face, which appeared as if he was trying to portray some kind of toughness. "What can I do for y'all today?" Jeff asked.

"Jeff, our family loves the sports of motocross and supercross. My wife and I have been riding together since before our marriage began and have raised our kids, you would think, right from birth to ride with us," Brady began.

"That's cool; I like to see a family with your kind of passion for the sport that I love so much," Jeff said to the small group.

"There's more. Our boy here just turned 11 years old the other day, and like the rest of us, he loves to ride."

"That's awesome buddy," Jeff said as he extended his fist in the boy's direction to offer a fist bump, "have you had a chance to demo any of our bikes and track today?"

Brady answered before the boy could, "no, we haven't done that today, we are confident your bikes and track are in excellent shape, and we have our own equipment we brought with us."

"Oh," Jeff answered, trying not to be offensive to the prospective clients, "I'm sorry, but we are not set up yet to allow free ride time. I appreciate that you have your own bikes, but for insurance purposes, we can't let you on the track right now."

"We understand completely, that is not what our intentions were. You see, we have noticed that our son, even as a very young child, has a natural ability on the motorcycle. He was riding and keeping up with us at a very young age. He has entered a few youth races in our home state and cleaned up every time. We feel like he is somewhat of a prodigy in the sport," Brady said proudly.

"Is that right?" Jeff said, looking at the boy.

Brady continued, "I know you have probably heard that before. I realize that all parents think their kids are the best at everything they do, but we are so sure of it, that, when we heard you were going to be opening a facility, we sold our house, packed up our things, and made plans to move out here for some year-round access to your expertise."

"Wow! You did all that before seeing the place?" Jeff said with surprise.

"It's not the facility we are interested in, it's you," Brady said as he pointed his finger at Jeff's chest.

"Well, thank you. I appreciate your confidence." Jeff was trying to figure out a way to tell them he was unsure he could meet their needs. He never intended to take anyone on for individualized training, except for Kara. He was unsure his facilities were suitable for what they had in mind. So he went ahead and asked them, "I'm not sure what I have designed here will meet your expectations. What, exactly, did you have in mind?"

Brady answered quickly and confidently, "We would like you to train our son full-time. We have made arrangements for him to attend one of the local private schools for his regular education, but other than that, we will fit our schedules to what you need, so you can train him as much as possible."

"Again, I appreciate your confidence in me, but I have to be honest; that level of training is not what I had in mind. I have not thought about what would be involved, nor how much the costs to my program and what the charges to you, as the client, would be," Jeff said.

"Don't worry about the charges. We are prepared to pay whatever you feel necessary. I own a number of successful restaurants back home and planned to open some more out here in Texas. The money is not an issue. Can we count on you to take care of him?" Brady extended his hand like he was a used car dealer trying to finalize a sale.

Jeff turned to the boy and asked, "Is that what you want?"

"Yes, sir," the young boy answered politely.

"What is your name buddy?" Jeff asked him.

"My name is Angus Stewart," he responded, "but everybody calls me Danger."

"Did you say Danger?" Jeff released a small chuckle, "That's cool."

"Yes, Danger is my middle name," he responded without hesitation, like he had done it hundreds of times.

Jeff looked at Brady and Candace, who were just smiling, and said, "Danger, huh? That's super cool."

"We thought you might like that," Candice said.

Jeff then looked back at Danger and said, "Well, Danger. Will you give me a day or two to think about this, come up with a plan to present to you and your parents and get back to you?"

Danger just smiled as Brady answered the question, "That would be great!" Then he pointed out to the field to the very large motorhome and trailer, "That rig over there is our temporary home, we will be at the RV park outside of town, but my cell phone number is 555–1234. We look forward to hearing from you."

Just as the family had turned to walk away, Kara approached Jeff after answering her own set of questions, signing a couple autographs, which she loved to do, and getting cleaned up a little. She asked Jeff, "Who were they?"

"They are a family that moved here because they want me to train their son," Jeff answered.

"They moved here for you?" Kara sounded very surprised, "Why would they do that?"

"Apparently they feel like their son is the best young rider in the country and they want me to train him full-time," Jeff said, looking at Kara to see her reaction.

Kara laughed, "I'll race him!"

"I bet you would, little miss fearless!" Jeff extended his hand for a high five and Kara responded accordingly, jumping and slapping his open palm.

"What is that kid's name?" Kara asked, gesturing with her head toward the parking fields, as she was looking in the distance at his family getting in their motorhome.

"Oh, you're gonna love this," Jeff paused and said, "wait for it…" Another pause, and then he said, "his name is Danger."

Kara laughed, "Danger? Really?" she said with a smirk on her face.

"Ya, I know. Apparently that is his middle name and that is what they call him," Jeff was smiling and noticeably amused while informing Kara of this information.

Kara turned and walked away, she felt a kind of jealousy feeling she was unfamiliar with. She didn't even know this boy, but she sensed that her training time with Jeff was soon going to be interrupted even more than she anticipated with the opening of this new training facility.

The following day, Kara and Greg went out of town for the rest of the week to spend some father daughter time together since Greg had taken the whole week off to make sure he didn't miss Kara's riding demonstration at the grand opening of RRA.

Jeff and Courtney, on the other hand, spent the next few days organizing all the info they had received regarding potential and signed students and discussing what they thought Jeff could do for Danger and his family.

Chapter 19 - The Mermaid

"Why do they call you the mermaid?" a young spectator, who looked to be about five or six years old, asked Kara, as he was tugging on her jersey.

It was the opening day of the biggest event Kara and Danger had been involved in since their riding careers began five years earlier. It was an event where they were the main attraction. Motocross fans had come from all over the state, and the states surrounding them to see the events of the weekend. They were in the same stadium where Jeff had his accident that changed his life forever.

Kara's thoughts had been all over in the days leading up to this event. She had never received so much attention. She had even been offered a big sponsorship through Revved Up energy drinks. She was wearing all their gear; the riding boots, pants, jersey, hats, and helmets. The little boy inquiring as to her nickname was not at all interested in any of that. He was fascinated with her for who she had become as an individual racer, the mermaid is what they called her in the dirt bike world.

"Is this your first time at a big race?" she asked the young boy.

"No, my dad has taken me to lots of races," he responded very matter-of-fact.

"Oh, okay, then," Kara was amused by the young fan. "Have you seen any of my jumps?"

"The jumps are my favorite part!" the boy said as he made a jumping gesture with his hand.

"Mine, too," Kara said with a smile. "You watch carefully today, and when it is my turn to do some jumping, watch the tricks I do. I think you will be able to figure out why I have the new nickname, the mermaid."

"Will you sign my shirt?" The boy turned around and displayed the signatures that he had already collected, the biggest one being Dangers.

"That is just like him," she mumbled under her breath, "he always thinks he has to be the biggest and the best."

Kara said to the boy, "Give me just a second, I am going to get my biggest, blackest, marker. Is that okay?"

"Ya," he said.

Kara returned in just a couple minutes and drew a picture of a mermaid jumping over Danger's name and signed her name to it, even bigger and boulder than Danger had signed his. She was laughing to herself as she did. Then she sent the boy on his way with his dad, "I better finish getting ready for the races," she said, "have a fun day!" She had always been so kind and accommodating to her fans. She felt like one of them and she always wanted them to feel like she was just like them too.

Kara turned and looked over at Jeff, who had been listening to the conversation while he was prepping the bikes. He seemed to know exactly what she was thinking and he simply gave her a nod. She then looked back over at the young boy, as he was walking away, and said, "Hey kid, wait a second."

The boy and his dad walked back to her and his dad said, "What is it?"

"Why don't the two of you follow me out onto the track right now and I will take a quick practice run," Kara suggested.

"Awesome!" said the boy, "Is that okay, Dad?"

With Dad's approval, they followed Kara as she idled her bike out to the track and showed them where they could stand, trackside, for just a few minutes. The little boy's eyes, as well as his dad's, were as big as they could be.

"You just stand here for a bit, and I will show you why they call me the mermaid," Kara gave the boy a high five.

Then he put his arms up over his head, and he yelled, "YES!"

Kara then proceeded to take a couple laps around the track to get the feel of the dirt and its grooves. Then she stopped at one end of the stadium and looked over at the boy and his dad, and gave them a wave. She revved her engine, spun out her rear tire, and took off toward the main jump, near the center of the arena. She approached the jump perfectly, and got just the right lift off the top. When she did, she started into her trick, letting go of the bike when she was in the air, just like the Superman trick, but instead of keeping her body straight after tugging the rear of the bike to float back to the front, she put her arms out in front of her like she was diving into some water and waved her body front to back like a fish swimming through the water, utilizing her double jointed knees for extra effect and curvature.

After she landed, she rode back over to where her new friends were watching her and said, "Well, what did you think of that?"

They were both holding their hands up for a high five, and the boy said, "That was cool, you looked just like a flying fish, like a mermaid!"

"Yep, that's what they say," Kara said to them. "Thanks for cheering me on. It's fans like you that make all the hard work worthwhile. I'm going to keep practicing and warming up, I hope the two of you enjoy the rest of the show."

Chapter 20 - Boys Need to be Beaten

Fifteen minutes later, Kara was ready to race. Jeff had just finished double checking her bike and making sure it was ready to go. She gave it a kick, revved the engine, and took off to the staging area. She pulled in right alongside Danger, who turned to say something to her, but as he did, she revved her engine, over and over again, and made a signal to her ear that she was not able to hear him. Danger made a fake laughing gesture, and turned off his bike, reaching over to turn Kara's off as well, but when he did, she swatted his hand away, like it was a fly.

This type of playful angst between the two of them was very common. Neither of them really meant anything by it. They had been training together for nearly 5 years now, and had moved past being rivals to being pretty good friends and training partners. It wasn't always that way, Kara really struggled for the first year or so when Jeff started training Danger full-time. She was still very young and she had a hard time understanding that Jeff could give her just as much training and still be able to train Danger too. The thing that bothered her the most, though, was how much he would come home and talk about the things Danger was learning in his private lessons and how great a rider he was. She experienced a lot of jealousy through the years and talked to her Grandma and Courtney a lot about the feelings she was having, and the hard time she was having with sharing Jeff's attention. They encouraged her to try and be Danger's friend so they could work together to make each other better, but Kara never felt like Danger was interested in that and she felt uncomfortable trying to get him to be her friend.

It wasn't until she was about 12 years old that things started to change, and in a very big way. Danger was an excellent rider and everyone knew it. He rarely, if ever, lost a race. He would even ride in higher age divisions, and still come away with first place trophies to show off to Kara. She had grown so tired of it until one day, after a long talk with her grandmother, Helen, she changed her entire attitude of the situation. She will never forget what her grandma said to her that day.

"Sometimes, my dear Kara, we can try and try and try to get along with someone through being nice, and it never seems to work," her grandma began to explain.

"So what else is there, should I try being mean to him?" Kara asked sincerely.

"No," Helen paused for a moment, "I think what might get through to a boy like Danger, who is so into being tough and macho, is if you beat him at what he does best."

"But I can't beat him Grandma," Kara said with emphatic frustration.

"Now Kara, you know that your dad, your grandpa and I, and Jeff and Courtney have never told you that you could not do something. Why would you say now that you can't beat Danger?" Helen said in a loving, but firm tone.

"He hardly ever loses, that's why. No one ever beats him! The only times he has not won have been when there was a mechanical problem with his bike or something out of his control," Kara said with a sigh, "and that doesn't count!"

"Now I would bet that is not true. I am sure he has been beaten at some point in his life," Grandma said with a smile.

"Not since I have known him," Kara's voice was noticeably downtrodden, sounding sad, "How am I supposed to just all of a sudden beat him in a race?"

"Does Danger know how to swim?" Helen asked.

"I don't know, but I bet he does. What does that have to do with anything?" Kara answered with another question.

"You should invite him to come out with us on the boat one Saturday and show him that he is not the best at everything," Helen had a grin as she continued, "you can first show him that when it comes to swimming, there is no one better than you…"

"Ya," Kara smiled wide, "I could kick his butt at swimming!"

"Well, that is not the end of it. After you show him how good you are at swimming, you need to talk to Jeff and ask him to show you every little thing you could work on or do differently to have the best chance of beating Danger at what he does best. Then you work your tail off until you master those skills and eventually, you will surprise the socks off that boy," Helen made a gesture with her fist clenched and swung her arm across in front of her.

They both laughed.

Helen continued, "He will notice you then and I think a lot will change between the two of you."

Kara did just what her Grandma suggested. After taking Danger and his family out on the boat with her dad one weekend and showing him how she could swim, she spent the next several months working harder than she had ever before on the techniques and procedures Jeff was teaching her to become a better motocross racer. She was even spending extra time doing strength and endurance training so her body could be as strong as possible. The nice thing about that was that swimming really helped her build extra strength and conditioning. And she loved to swim, so she was putting more time in at the local pool as well, getting faster and stronger.

It was late in the racing year, when she and Danger were about 12 and 13 years old, respectively, when she finally accomplished her goal. She beat him. It wasn't a total kick butt like she had imagined, but she did beat him.

It was around the final corner of the track on the final lap, she had been hanging with him the entire race, something she had never done before, waiting for him to get nervous and make a mistake, which, of course, was rare for him. When they came around the final corner, it happened. He looked over his shoulder to see where she was, and she was not there. Kara had been anticipating him looking over his inside shoulder, so she went to his outside. This caused him to look even farther, turning his head nearly all the way around to look for her, which caused him to slow down slightly to avoid losing control. This was the distraction Kara had been waiting for. Danger hit a rut and his bike threw him off balance. He was able to recover, but it was too late, Kara had passed him and was not looking back. She was giving her bike all the power she could as she cut in front of him, showering him with a spray of dirt. She headed straight for the finish jump, she could see the checkered flag; it was practically calling her name. She was overwhelmed with excitement and as she hit that jump, sailing into the air, she performed her favorite trick, The Superman, because it made her feel so free. She felt she was flying for several minutes as she reached her arms out to the side, she even closed her eyes sensing where the bike flying below her was. It was an incredible feeling, a feeling that she had been waiting for since the day she met that Danger boy.

Danger was not far behind. He completed the final jump in second place and for the first time in a long time, he did not perform any fancy trick as he went over the finish line jump. He landed and rode straight to Kara and Jeff, who were celebrating her win.

Kara saw him and thought to herself, "I bet he is so mad!"

Danger locked the brakes on his rear tire and slid right up next to her. To Kara's surprise he was smiling and extended his fist for a congratulatory fist bump "nice race," he said, sounding very genuine.

"Thanks!" Kara said as she hit his fist with hers.

"That was an awesome move on the last corner, I never expected you to go high side," Danger said.

"I know; that's why I did," Kara said with a grin. She could feel the change in their relationship happening immediately, like it was a seedling that had just broken through the dirt to see the sunlight for the first time.

"Believe it or not," Danger, said, "I have been expecting you to beat me in one of these races for the last few months. I have been watching you train and seeing how hard you have been working. You are an excellent rider and deserve to win as much as anyone else on the track."

Kara leaned over her bike toward him and sprung her arms up and wrapped them around his neck, nearly knocking him off his bike in the process. It was their first hug. It was their first sign of affection of any kind, other than fist bumps.

Danger slowly and hesitantly returned her hug by putting his hands on her waist. It was awkward for both of them, but along with the results of the race, it changed everything. Kara no longer felt a distance between her and Danger.

It was at that moment, that fans and race reporters started rushing in and crowding their space. Kara, Danger, and Jeff started to answer all the questions and give autograph requests. As they did, Kara and Danger looked at each other with a mutual respect neither of them had ever felt before. They both felt it, a feeling like they were now, not only teammates, but friends too.

"Who wants a Revved Up?" Jeff shouted as the crowd responded with the roar of cheers. He had renewed his sponsorship with Revved Up as the trainer for riders like Danger and Kara. They both knew that he had said it, this time, out of contract obligation, and were not a bit surprised when the next thing he said to them when the crowd began to disperse was, "Now, let's go get something fun to eat; who wants pizza?" He paused briefly, and spoke softer as he leaned toward the two of them and said with a smile, "Without the Revved Up."

They all laughed together for a minute.

Then Danger said, "Thanks, but I can't make it out with you guys tonight."

"Why not?" Asked Jeff as Greg approached them and interrupted before Danger could answer.

"What's going on?" He said as more of a statement than a question, immediately hugging Kara and congratulating her on her win. "I thought you said that kid couldn't be beaten," he playfully jabbed Danger in the arm with his finger, "I knew you could do it, honey, that was an excellent race!"

Then Jeff said, "We are going to all go out for pizza, but he can't join us."

"Oh, come on buddy, come out with all of us," Greg said to him, "don't be a poor sport because of the girl beatin' up on you today."

"Dad!" Exclaimed Kara with embarrassment.

"I'm just messing with him, he knows it," Greg said to her.

"It's cool," Danger said, "it's not the race at all. I just can't come tonight. I want to, but I can't."

"Where is your dad?" Jeff asked, "I will talk to him, I'm sure he'll be fine if you hang out with us for a couple hours. We will bring you home."

"No really, I want to go out with you guys and normally my dad would be fine with it. We just have other plans tonight," Danger said as he looked down at the ground.

"A big dinner at one of your dad's restaurants?" Kara said jokingly.

"Funny," Danger was matching her sarcasm, "but no. We are not eating out…"

Kara, Greg, and Jeff just looked at Danger, waiting for further explanation. He was obviously hesitant to tell them what it was that interfered with a celebration of Kara's first major win.

"My dad's brothers are in town, with my cousins, and we are going out on the boat," Danger explained.

"Boat?" Kara asked, "I've never heard you mention a boat before."

"Ya, me either," added Jeff.

"We don't mean to interrogate you," Greg said, "but it would be pretty late to be going out on the Gulf by the time you drive home. What would you guys do out there that late at night?"

Danger's Dad, Brady, was just then walking up and noticed that his son was seemingly surrounded by the group, and said to him, "What's up dude?"

"Nothing dad," Danger said nervously, "these guys are going out for pizza."

Brady turned and put his arm around danger, pulling him into his chest and both of them turning from the group. "You didn't tell them what we were doing, did you?" He said quietly.

"Of course not, Dad, Kara's dad is a fisherman," Danger said in his ear.

"Brady," Jeff spoke up, "Danger was just saying he can't come to get pizza with us. It's no problem."

"Not at all," Greg said, "but I'm just curious what you guys are going to do so late at night out on the gulf, especially with kids with you."

"Don't worry about it man," Brady was a nice man, but did a good job of putting on a tough image, "we're going fishing."

"No, you're not," said Greg.

"Dad," Kara said abruptly, "stop, please."

"What do you mean," Brady said to Greg, "no, we're not?"

Greg said, "What, exactly, are you going to fish for in the dark, close enough to land to not be gone all night long or more?"

"Whatever we can. Don't worry about it, it's mostly just for the fun of being together with my brothers." Brady grabbed the handlebars of Danger's bike, "Let's go," he said to Danger, and they both turned and walked away.

Jeff and Greg looked at each other and Greg said, "That was weird. There isn't anything you can legally fish for with any success this late at night."

"No doubt, but let's just go eat. I'm starving!" Jeff knew Greg was passionate about his occupation, as was Kara about sea life, and he could tell Greg didn't feel right about whatever Danger and his family were going to be doing that evening out on the Gulf.

"Hmm," Greg, uttered, "ya, let's go eat."

Chapter 21 - The Night Before

"Do you have everything ready for tomorrow morning?" Asked Greg as he was saying good night to Kara.

"I do dad, I think I am already," Kara replied, followed up by her usual good night ritual, "You're going to come back, right?"

It was Sunday night and just like any other week, Greg had to go out to sea in the morning and Kara would be staying with Jeff and Courtney for a few days to a week; however long it took him and his crew to catch their weekly allotted maximum.

It was the second week after school let out for the summer, and the two of them had spent last week vacationing on the West Coast so Kara was not going out with the crew this week. Kara loved swimming at the California beaches. Greg had planned many things for them to do during their trip, but Kara loved the swimming part so much, they had scratched some of those other plans for more time at the beach. Some boys she met the second day had taught her how to surf and she loved it. Greg let her stay out till dark that night, and keep catching wave after wave. It wasn't the same to her as back home. The tide and waves just seemed different to her, but the week flew by.

Even with the fun she had had during last week, Kara's mind was still overwhelmed with excitement for tomorrow. It was the first day of the high school swim team tryouts; she wanted so much to make the varsity team, but knew she had to do her best as a freshman because of the talent the other girls had, especially those who had been on the team for a year or two. She tried to put her mind on something else, "Dad, when can I stay by myself at our house while you are out working?"

"Whoa," Greg was caught off guard by the question, "where did that question come from? I thought you liked staying with your aunt and uncle."

"I do," Kara paused, trying to think of a good reason she had just blurted out a totally unexpected question, "I just feel like it is a lot of work for them and a lot of work for you to have to arrange everything with them, and even up all the bills and whatever else you have to do."

Greg put his hand on Kara's forearm and said, "Honey, you don't have to worry about those things. Jeff and I don't. He and Courtney love having you stay with them. You are like a daughter to them and they have never, not once in your life, said anything negative about you staying here. They love you as their own child."

"I know they do, but I feel like it would be easier on everyone if I just stayed at our house," Kara said, even though she realized she was still too young.

"Well," Greg grinned, "that is nice of you to think of the feelings of others, but you are not nearly old enough to stay at home alone while I am gone for the week."

"When will I be?" Kara said, now very interested in what she had to look forward to.

"Let's aim for 18 for now," Greg answered.

"That's more than three years though," Kara said with a plea and sigh.

"I know," Greg knew Kara was a good girl and had shown tremendous maturity throughout her life. He fully expected her to be able to stay on her own anytime now, but also knew she was now facing the challenges of high school, which can be extremely trying on a teenage girl. He continued, "Let's just look at how things are going from time to time and make the decision together as we go. I like the idea of you having Jeff, and especially Courtney, to talk to during your high school years."

"Okay dad, it's not that big a deal anyway. I was just wondering," Kara said softly, as if she was acting sad.

"I love you, honey. You are an amazing girl, and I am very proud of you. You are going to do great tomorrow, but you need to get to sleep so you will be well rested to perform your best," Greg gave her a kiss on the forehead.

"Thanks dad, I love you too. I'm trying not to be too nervous," Kara said, still speaking softly.

"Kara, you are the best swimmer that school will ever know. You are going to blow their minds, just like you continually blow my mind. Just relax and swim and you will be fine," Greg said passionately.

Kara smiled, laid-back in her bed and pulled her covers up to her neck.

"Good night girl," Greg said, as he turned out the light, "sleep well."

No sooner had her dad closed the door, but her alarm clock was sounding at 4:30 AM. She rolled over and turned it off with no desire at all to hit snooze or sleep anymore. "I don't know whose idea it is to have swim tryouts at five in the morning, but I am not going to be late," she quietly told herself. Then it was off to get some breakfast.

To Kara's surprise, Courtney was already in the kitchen making some breakfast.

"How's the swim champ this morning?" Courtney asked Kara as she turned the corner and had a look of surprise to see her aunt up.

"I haven't even tried out yet. I'm not exactly a swim champ," Kara said with little confidence.

"I know, but I have seen you swim and I know how good you are. It's the only thing you do better than ride and I don't think I need to remind you of how good you are on the dirtbike, little miss fifth place in the country." There had recently been a release of the top motocross riders in the teenage division ages 12 to 18 Kara ranked fifth among all participants, male and female.

"That's nice of you to say, but I still need to try out and get picked for the team," Kara said.

"Girl, they're not only going to pick you, but they are going to make y'all team captain as well," Courtney said, with an extra southern drawl.

"Very funny," Kara reached for a slice of toast and honey. "Thanks for making breakfast."

"You're welcome, I'm happy to do it. Now let's get you fed and get you over to the pool!" Courtney said enthusiastically.

Chapter 22 - Tryouts

"Hey Kara," said Julie, one of Kara's closest friends, who had already been swimming when Kara arrived at the school pool.

"Hi, Jules, how's the water?" Kara inquired.

"I only took a quick lap or two to get warmed up, but it seems fine to me, nothing wrong with the temperature anyway," Julie said, noticeably nervous.

"Fine for you or fine for me?" Kara joked.

"Ha ha, I know you like the water colder than most people. I think you'll like it," Julie answered as she was toweling off.

Kara threw her towel over to the side of the pool by some others and stretched her hands down to her toes, bending at the waist. She was consciously trying not to let her knees bend backward. Although she was okay with being double jointed, she did not know how others would perceive it. She didn't want anyone to accuse her of having some kind of unfair advantage. Then she dove into the water and swam, feeling the water rush by her, like a fish swimming upstream. She loved the feeling she had when she was slicing through the water, kicking those legs, swinging those arms over and over, pulling the water with her hands. She felt a total power when she was in the water, like she had control of all her surroundings. It was then that all the anxiety she had been feeling about tryouts just up and left her, she felt at peace. She knew everything was going to be fine.

When she finished a couple laps, she climbed out of the pool to find the varsity swim coach standing right there by Julie, but Kara did not hear what they were saying. Then, as she was drying off, he walked over to her and said, "That wasn't your first time in the water, was it?"

Kara's mind was racing; she could not believe he was even talking to her! Tryouts had not even started! What was she going to say? What exactly did he want or mean?

So she bravely gathered a smile, and simply said, "No, sir, it wasn't."

"You can just call me coach," he said to her.

"Okay, coach," Kara appropriately responded.

"Where have you been swimming?" He asked.

Kara thought that was a strange question and did not really know what he meant. "I swim everywhere I can. My dad said I was born swimming."

"I think you might truly have been, from what I just saw, but what I meant is what team have you been swimming with?" the coach clarified.

"Team?" Kara asked sincerely, but she also felt confused, "I have never been on a team."

"Really?" The coach said surprised, "you look like a seasoned pro, like you've been very well coached."

"Thank you, Coach, but I have only been swimming for fun, my whole life, and I am looking forward to trying to swim competitively." Kara paused, hoping she didn't sound too confident, "I mean, if I make the team that is."

"If you always swim like I just saw, you'll not only make the team, but be the last leg of our varsity relay team too," The coach paused, and then asked, "What's your name?"

"Kara Landers," Kara replied, trying to contain the excitement within her. She felt like she had just won a major motocross race and didn't know what else to say, so she just stood there, with a huge smile plastered on her face.

"Well, Kara, how about we get all these swimmers lined up and start some tryouts?" The coach spoke like he was asking permission, but she knew he was just making a statement.

Then he walked away as he blew his whistle.

Kara turned to Julie and they both grabbed each other by the hands and started jumping up and down, laughing, and quietly screaming to each other.

For the entire tryouts, Kara just swam. She swam like she was in the sea, totally comfortable and at peace. She didn't feel like she had to impress anybody, so she just swam like she loved to, because she did.

She was the only girl trying out that day who had signed up to swim all of the different strokes, and when one of the assistant coaches asked her about it, to see if it was correct, Kara just said, "Yes, is that okay?"

"Sure it is, if that's what you want to do, but most of the kids just pick one or two they are strongest in and try out with those, then we work on adding the other strokes during the season and practices," the assistant coach replied.

"I don't really know which stroke I am strongest at," Kara said, "I just love to swim and know how to swim all the strokes, so I just thought I would do them all."

"Cool, and it looks like you are right so far, you're doing great," the assistant said, as she wrote something on her clipboard.

The tryouts continued until almost noon and then the coaches told the kids to look at the school website the following morning to see a list of who was selected for the team. Kara went home and told Courtney and Jeff all about it and called her dad to leave him a message he could get when they turned on their satellite devices in the evening. That night he called her from the boat, which he rarely did because of the cost. He told her how proud he was of her and that he just knew she was going to make the team.

Kara woke up before her alarm went off at 4:30 the next morning. She was so excited to check the tryout results; that excitement was thoroughly upheld when she saw her name listed on the varsity team. She let out a little yelp of joy. Then she kept reading, and saw something more...

The coach had posted some additional information following the names of those who made the team, and asked everyone to read it; it read:

"Congratulations to all those who were selected to each of the teams, I am very confident we will have a great year and be very competitive at the district and state levels. I'm sure some of you may have noticed that we had a couple swimmers this year that stood out above the rest, putting up exceptional times, and swimming like seasoned pros. One of them, Cru, you already know as our men's team captain from last year, but the other is a newcomer; a freshman girl. As a result, the coaching staff and I have discussed an opportunity to grow our program into something more resembling a collegiate swim team. We have decided to create a team position of student coach. We will select one male and one female to assist us in this new role. The two student coaches will be selected after they are interviewed by the coaching staff, and have agreed to the extra responsibilities. Once we have made our final selections, we will let you know who will be assuming these two new positions on the team. Thanks again to all of you who came to tryouts and congratulations to all who we will be working with this year. We will see you Monday morning at 5 AM!

Kara wasn't sure what to think of this idea of student coaches and really did not give it much thought. She was just excited to be on the team! Even though she was a freshman and the coaches had given her some extra attention at tryouts, she was not a prideful person, and did not make the connection or assumption that it might be her they were interested in. After all, she had never even been on a competitive swim team before, so she went about her day, and didn't give it another thought.

Chapter 23 - Student Coach

Later in the day, when Kara was at the track working out with Jeff, Danger rode up to the side of her bike and said, "Missed you yesterday, how did swim tryouts go?" He had a little grin on his face, like he knew something she didn't.

"What's with the smirk?" Kara asked.

"What smirk?" Danger replied, almost laughing.

"You totally have a stupid looking smile on your face, like you're trying to hide something from me," Kara said in a playful, but annoyed tone.

"Whatever, you think you are so smart!" Danger replied.

"Danger, I've known you a while now, and I can tell when you're trying to hide something or a joke about something," Kara insisted.

"Oh, come on; just tell me about tryouts already. Did you make the team?" Danger countered.

"Yes, I made the team!" Kara said loudly.

Danger reached his hand out to give Kara a fist bump, which she obliged slowly, and he asked, "But does that mean you won't be hanging around here so much?"

"You wish!" Kara said emphatically. Then she kick started her bike, stepped it into gear, popped the clutch, and threw dirt all over Danger's bike as she took off to hit some laps.

Danger followed her lead and trailed her around the track a few times until Jeff signaled them in to give them some instruction for the evening training.

As Kara was getting her bike and equipment put away, her phone rang, but she did not answer it because she was not expecting a call from anyone and she did not recognize the number. When she was finished and headed home, she listened to the message the caller had left. It was a call from the school swim coach explaining that he and the other coaches wanted to meet with her and asked her to call him back.

She waited until she got home, and she nervously made the call.

"Hello," said the coach's deep voice on the other end of the call.

"Is this coach Anderson?" Kara asked softly.

"Yes it is. Is this Kara I'm speaking with?" the coach replied.

Kara was familiar with proper grammar, but still felt intimidated by his speech and tone, "Yes, it's Kara Landers here."

"Well hello, Kara!" His tone completely changed and he now sounded very happy and fun, "How are you this evening?"

"Good," she said, then pausing, hoping he would speak next, but he didn't, "I got your message and just wanted to call you back."

"I'm glad you did. You probably already know why I want to talk to you, right?" he said clearly.

Kara hesitated, thinking about what to say. She still had the track on her mind. She was excited for swim practice to start next week and very excited to swim varsity, but swimming was such a huge, natural part of her life, she hadn't been putting too much thought into it, "I'm sorry sir, I don't."

"Now Kara, didn't I tell you to just call me coach?" he said with a little laugh.

"Yes, Coach, sorry," Kara corrected herself.

"Don't be sorry. You are very polite, but I feel very comfortable with just being called Coach." He continued, sounding surprised or confused, "Are you sure you don't know why I'm calling you?"

"No coach," Kara said.

"Well, okay then," coach Anderson released a small audible sigh, "I guess I'll have to surprise you then. Did you read my statement on the swim tryouts website this morning?"

"Yes, I did," Kara said.

"What do you think?" the coach asked her.

"You said some really nice things. It was well worded," Kara replied, but in a confused way, sincerely not knowing why the coach was calling her or asking her the questions.

"No, Kara, I mean about the student coaching. What do you think about our idea to have student coaches?" he clarified.

"I think it's a fine idea," Kara said, still confused. She did not assume in the least that the coach was asking her to be a student coach.

"Kara, the coaching staff and I would like you to be a student coach," he said invitingly.

"Why me?" Kara asked sincerely, "I've never done anything but swim for fun, mostly with my family. I don't know anything about being a student swim coach. Or really anything about swimming competitively."

Coach Anderson replied confidently and kindly, "You don't have to know anything about being a coach. You just need to be a great swimmer, and you are one of the best I've ever seen. You need to be willing to give some advice to your teammates occasionally and help them improve their swimming abilities."

The phone was silent. Not an awkward silence, though, Kara was thinking about what had just been proposed to her and the coach knew that and allowed her the time to think.

After about a minute, the coach said, "Kara, what do you think about being a student coach? We would love it if you would help the team out in a way we feel will be a great benefit to everyone on the team and even more beneficial to your future with swimming."

"Can I think about it?" Kara asked hesitantly.

The coach replied positively, "Of course you can. Take your time and make sure it is something you would like to do…"

Kara did not let the coach finish his sentence before she said excitedly, "Okay, I will do it. I will be a student coach."

"Are you sure? You just said you wanted to think about it," Coach Anderson asked with a little laugh.

"I did. I think it would be fun, but I really don't know what to do so I guess you and the other coaches will be there to help out, right?" Kara said.

"Of course we will!" Coach answered with excitement, "and so will Cru, our other student coach. Do you know Cru?" he responded.

"I don't," Kara hesitated, "I mean, I heard his name a couple of times at tryouts, and read what you wrote about him on your website, but no, I don't know him."

"I think you'll like him a lot. He is an amazing swimmer. He swims like nothing you have ever seen before. He has never been beaten, and frankly, I don't think he ever will be beaten. The way he swims is…" the coach stopped, "well, I won't go on about him. You are a great swimmer too, and I look forward to the two of you working with us."

"Thanks Coach!" Kara said enthusiastically.

"Thank you, Kara," he said, "and we will see you bright and early Monday morning."

Kara hung up and put down her phone.

"Courtney!" Kara yelled through the house, so excited that she felt like doing cartwheels down the hallway, "Courtney!" She heard no reply, "Jeff! Are you guys home?"

Kara heard the garage door to the kitchen area open and close.

"Kara," Courtney replied from the kitchen, "are you calling us? We were out in the garage."

Kara ran into the kitchen, "Yes, yes I was. Get Jeff, I have to tell you something totally exciting."

"Let's just go out there," Courtney suggested, "Jeff has something he wants to show you too."

The two of them went out to the garage, where Jeff had what looked like a motorcycle, covered up with an old army tarp, but Kara paid no attention to that. Jeff was always working on something in the garage.

"You know I told you guys that I made the varsity team, right?" Kara began.

They both nodded and agreed, "Sure you did, what's going on now that has you doubly excited?" Courtney asked.

"Well, the coaching staff said on their website that they had decided to make a new leadership position on the team this year for a couple of the student swimmers." Kara then explained what the website said about the student coaches, and then continued, "so guess who just got off the phone with the varsity head coach?"

"What? Why?" Jeff exclaimed and then asked rhetorically, "Did he ask you to be the student coach? That wouldn't surprise me a bit, you oversized fish!"

Kara grinned so big it nearly wrapped around her ears. She did not have to say a word to confirm Jeff's question in the affirmative.

"Woo hoo!" He shouted, "Way to go, girl!"

"That is awesome honey," said Courtney as she came over, and hugged Kara, "you are going to do a great job, I just know it!"

"I am kind of nervous about it, to tell you the truth," said Kara to Courtney.

"Oh Kara," Courtney said with compassion, "you are the best swimmer I've ever seen. There is no doubt you could share your knowledge of the water with the other teammates; and you are such a nice person, always able to make friends easily. You don't have anything to worry about."

Kara said quietly, "But I am younger than every other girl on the team. I am the only freshman girl on the varsity team. Don't you think the other girls will disrespect me for trying to coach them?"

"I doubt it," Courtney told her, "I bet if you just take it easy, don't start trying to coach them or anything at first, just try to be friendly. Then let them see you swim." Courtney put her arm around Kara and pulled her close so she could talk softer, closer to her ear, "Kara, when they see you cutting through the water like you are some sort of motorboat or something, they will have nothing but questions for you on how they can get to be an amazing swimmer like you."

"You really think so?" Kara asked sincerely, "I just don't know anything about coaching."

"Remember, just be their friend and you'll be fine. I promise," Courtney told her assuredly.

"Thank you Courtney," Kara said, as she leaned into her Aunt's hug.

"For sure, honey," Courtney pulled back from the hug, then put both her arms on Kara's shoulders, and leaned down toward her face and said, "I can't wait to see you compete. That is going to be so exciting."

"Me too," came a voice from the yard. Kara thought it sounded like her dad, but why would he be here after only being out to sea for two days, she thought.

Then Greg stepped into the garage light, and Kara ran to him to give him big hugs, "Dad, your home!"

Chapter 24 - The Street Bike

As Kara was hugging her dad, he said to her, "Congratulations honey, I knew you would make the team! And Courtney is right, you're going to do a great job as a student coach."

"How do you know about that?" Kara asked him.

"Your coach called me last night and asked me if I thought it would be okay to offer you the opportunity," her Dad replied.

"Oh cool, that makes sense. Is that why you're home early?" Kara said.

Greg grabbed his daughter by the hand, leading her over to the tarp covered object on the other side of the garage, "Well, the good news is that we had a huge day yesterday, as well as this morning, almost catching our weekly max in just two days."

"That's good. Super cool dad," Kara congratulated him.

"So I wanted to come home and celebrate the good news about swimming, and I also wanted to be here with Jeff when he shows you what we got for you." Greg smiled and turned to look at Jeff, giving him a wink.

"What?" Kara asked with surprise, "what are you talking about?"

Greg looked at Jeff again and then turned back to Kara, "Okay, a couple months ago, I was talking to Jeff about what you could drive to school when you are able to get licensed to drive. Now, I know Jeff has been letting you drive one of his older team trucks around the back roads and you are always welcome to drive my old beater car, but I didn't think either of those suits your style."

"Dad," Kara stopped him, "you know I don't care about style. I'll drive whatever there is. It doesn't matter to me. Plus, you know I like that old 80's T-bird, and when you fix it up, it's going to be one hot ride."

"I know, honey, you have always been very independent in the way you dress and act, not caring what others think, just being yourself, and I think that is totally cool," Greg said as he put his arm on her shoulder.

"I love that about you, too, Kara," Courtney agreed.

Greg continued, "So Jeff had told me that one of the motorcycle companies he works with through sponsorships and stuff has always told him they would do just about anything for him; and as we talked about it, we thought it would be cool to get you a street bike to ride to school, your practices, and around town."

"WHAT!? Are you kidding me right now, dad?" Kara jumped as she reacted to her dad's recent revelation, "Is that what's under the tarp?"

When Kara said that, Jeff came over and took the tarp off the motorcycle in front of them, revealing a tricked out street bike.

"Aaaaaaaa!" Kara let out a scream and began jumping up and down with excitement. She was looking at a brand new, customized, street bike. It was mostly dark blue, but when a certain light hit the paint, it changed to a dark green color. The bike also had some custom art on the tank, it was a painting of her on her dirt bike, performing her signature trick; the artwork was done very professionally and she loved it. Underneath the art were the words "Mermaid Racing Team."

Kara was almost in shock. She had stopped jumping up and down as she looked over the bike, her jaw dropping closer and closer to the floor. "I can't believe this," she said, "this is the most beautiful bike I have ever seen! Is it really for me?"

Even with the success Kara had been experiencing as a dirt bike racer, and the money she got from endorsements and public appearances, she did not ever spend very much on herself. She put most of her earnings in savings for the future, and did a lot of work for charity whenever she could. Most people who met her for the first time would never guess how successful she was. She was very down to earth and humble about her success. So she would never expect to have something like this just given to her. She was truly in disbelief about it.

"Of course it's really yours," Greg said. "You deserve something you can call your own and be proud to ride." Then Greg stopped what he was saying because he could see the look Kara was giving him. It was a look like, "Dad, you know I do not like being the focus of any attention…" Those kinds of things were just simply not important to her. Greg continued, "You know, not proud to ride, that's not what I mean. That's not you. I just want you to have something nice, that is yours, that you can have for yourself."

"Thanks Dad. Thanks Jeff, I love it!" She looked down at the bike again and ran her hand along the leather seat and up across the gas tank "What's with the fancy paint?"

Jeff added, "I thought it was time for you to really start making your own name for yourself. Mermaid racing team is all you. It's your brand. What do you think?"

"Hmmm," Kara put her hand to her chin like she was really giving it some deep thought, but she was actually just messing with them. She loved it and thought it was perfect. "At least you didn't put a cheesy fishtail on me or something."

They all laughed.

"Uh, ya," Jeff said hesitantly as he looked at Greg, "that would've been pretty cheesy."

He knew that had been a topic of conversation between them. Jeff had wanted to do it, but Greg talked him out of it.

"When can I ride it?" Kara asked.

Greg answered her, "You can ride it now. In fact, I'll go for a ride with you."

Greg had never been much of a motorcycle rider. He was always just fine to support Jeff when they were boys and now he was in full support of Kara and her riding, so Kara was not sure what to think when her dad said he would go with her.

"Okay, I guess, Dad, which of Jeff's bikes is he going to let you ride?" Kara said in slight confusion with a funny look on her face.

"Ha ha, very funny little girl. I'll have you know that when I decided to have Jeff get you this new street bike, I asked him to get me one too, and I have been riding some here and there lately while you are out doing other things on the weekends," Greg said with pride.

"Awesome dad! But are you going to be able to keep up with me?" Kara joked.

"Oh geez, very funny again," Greg said as he lightly pushed Kara in the shoulder.

Jeff interrupted, "Kara, riding on the street is very different from riding in the dirt. Please take it easy at first, until you have a feel for the way the bike acts and reacts. You and your dad can learn street riding together."

Kara and Greg looked at each other with a smirk and Kara said, "Okay old man, let's do it. I've always wanted to go riding along the pier at night."

With that statement, Kara and Greg started their new bikes, pointed them to the street, and took off into the evening air together. The joy Kara was feeling right then, with everything that had happened over the past few days, was almost overwhelming. She began to cry with happiness as they headed out of town.

Chapter 25 - Not Much of a Fan

The very next morning, after having received what she thought was the greatest gift ever, she had one thing, and one thing only, on her mind: she wanted to show her new bike to Danger.

He was at the track, of course, working on his jumps when he noticed a small cloud of smoke coming from the parking lot near the shop. When he went over to see what was going on, he saw Kara turning and burning her rear tire on the pavement. She knew that would get his attention, but she had her helmet on, and he did not know it was her as she was spinning round and round.

As he approached the scene, she had stopped and the smoke started to clear. He noticed a ponytail out the back of the rider's helmet, matching the color of Kara's hair. "Kara?" He asked loudly with a confused tone, "is that you?"

She took off her helmet to reveal herself and said with a playful smile, "Hey Danger boy, do you want to go for a ride?"

"What. Is. That?" Danger asked slowly and pronounced as he completed a gasp.

"It's my new ride," Kara said with a smile, "Do you like it?"

"Well, I've never been much of a fan of street bikes, but that one is pretty cool," Danger said, trying to seem uninterested.

"Get on, I'll give you a ride," Kara said to him.

"Yeah, right," he chuckled, "you give me a ride? How about I give you a ride?"

"Oh, just get on the back and I'll show you how it's done," Kara insisted, turning her head away from him and revving her engine.

Danger hesitantly climbed on the back of Kara's street bike, and she took him for a ride down some of the back roads for a few minutes.

"Your hair is blowing in my face," Danger shouted from the back of the bike after a couple miles.

Kara laughed and flipped her head back and forth to make it flow even more into his face.

"No, seriously, I think you're going to make me blind," Danger joked. "Trade me places and let me drive on the way back."

Kara immediately pulled over: Secretly, that is what she wanted anyway. She liked the idea of giving him a ride, to show him that she could, but her feelings for him were starting to change. She wanted him to give her a ride. She wanted him to take control and show her that he could ride a street bike too. She wanted to sit behind him and hold on tight. She thought if she did that, it might get his attention and create feelings in him for her as well.

What Kara didn't know, though, is that she had had Danger's attention for a long time. Ever since the day she beat him on the dirt track, he had started looking at her and their friendship in a totally different way. It turns out Kara's grandma was more correct than she knew. Danger started to be aware of what Kara was doing and with whom, and had been watching her carefully for the last couple years. He didn't quite recognize what his feelings for her were until he felt her grab onto him tightly on the back of the bike that day. His heart was racing and his stomach was filled with butterflies. He wanted to ride for hours and hours that day, but he knew they had to get back to the track before Jeff got there, so he turned back and raced toward RRA.

When they returned to the track and started working out with Jeff, they both felt differently and couldn't stop looking at each other. Danger would look at Kara until she looked his way, then he would quickly turn his head. Then Kara would do the same thing. A couple of times, Kara started giggling about it, and Jeff said, "Kara, what's up with you today?"

"Nothing," she would say, "nothing at all. I'm fine."

"In fact," Jeff further inquired, "you're both acting a little weird. Is there something going on around here that I should know about?"

Kara and Danger looked at each other and smiled a cheesy smile and Danger replied, "No Jeff, seriously, nothings going on. Let's get back to work."

Kara was fine with Danger answering Jeff for both of them. She knew Jeff would take Danger seriously and drop it after that.

And with that said, the three of them went about their training as usual.

After training was over, Kara went back to her Uncle's house to gather her things, shower, and clean up as she did every other day, but this time after she was done, Courtney wanted to talk to her.

"Kara," Courtney said as she knocked on the bathroom door.

"Yeah Courtney, I'm just finishing getting dressed," Kara answered without opening the door.

Courtney said, "When you are out of there, come to the family room please. I want to talk to you."

Courtney did not sound angry or upset about anything, so Kara was puzzled, "What about?"

"Nothing major or urgent, I just want to talk to you," Courtney's voice was soft and kind.

"Okay, just a minute," Kara said, feeling at ease.

Kara was done in just a few minutes and went into the family room, where Courtney was watching TV. She turned it off when she saw Kara come into the room.

Courtney had a big cheesy grin on her face and Kara said bashfully, "Okay, what's up with the corny smile?"

"Jeff told me about practice today," Courtney said with bright eyes, still smiling.

Kara got a big cheesy grin on her face too and said, "What? What about practice today?"

"Why don't you tell me, lovebird?" Courtney said in a playful tone.

Kara gasped and they just looked at each other for a few seconds, smiling big smiles with eyes wide, like they were both trying so hard to keep a secret.

Then Kara said, "What does it feel like to fall in love?"

"Aaaahhhh," Courtney screamed quietly as to not create a big scene or alarm Jeff, "I knew it! I just knew it! I knew when Jeff told me the way you and Danger were acting today that something was up. He is just a dumb old guy when it comes to things like this, but I knew something was going on. I knew it! Now tell me everything."

"What did Jeff say?" Kara asked as she sat down close to Courtney.

"Oh, don't worry about that," Courtney said as she put her hand gently on Kara's forearm, "He just said that you and D were acting strange, like you had some joke between the two of you or something. He also told me that he saw you two on your new bike before practice and that Danger was driving."

"He did?" Kara said as her jaw dropped slowly and accentuated, "I didn't know he was even there yet. How embarrassing!"

"So what's going on Kara? You have to tell me," Courtney had a perma-smile.

"I don't know, exactly," Kara began, but she did not know how to express what she wanted to tell Courtney, "I mean, I just wanted to show him my new bike and so I took him for a ride and it was really, really fun!"

"So do you like him?" Courtney asked.

"Aaaahhh," Kara let out the same type of quiet scream Courtney just had, but with more of a grunting sound to it, "I don't know. He is cute and everything, but ever since I met him when we were little, we have been arch rivals. He was so mean to me sometimes. I swore I hated him."

There was a pause, and Courtney was just smiling ear to ear.

"Whahaat?" Kara said giggling and drawn out.

"Oh nothing," Courtney smirked and sarcastically said, "do you still hate him?"

"No, I don't still hate him. I stopped hating him when I beat him a few years back. In fact, that is when he stopped being mean to me and we started to get along a little better," Kara explained.

"So what's going on with you now? You just asked me what it is like to fall in love, so you have to start telling me more," Courtney adjusted her position on the couch to lean more toward Kara and sit a little closer, "You have to tell me more, girlie! Tell me more! Tell me more!" She casually chanted.

"Well," Kara was feeling so much excitement to tell someone, "the other day after Jeff and my Dad gave me the new bike, the only thing I could think about was showing it to Danger. At first, I thought I wanted to show it to him to brag that I could do something that he couldn't, but that thought left me faster than it hit me because I realized that I wanted to show him my new bike because he is my friend. I like him. I like being around him and I wanted him to be happy for me."

"Oh, Kara, that is so awesome and sweet!" Courtney said kindly.

Kara continued, "So I took it to show him and take him for a ride and when he got on the back and we started to go, I realized that I did not want to drive. I wanted him to give me a ride. I wanted to hold onto him tightly. So when we switched places and I was holding on like I imagined, it felt so good. I could feel the strength and security in his muscles. I could feel the confidence he had with the bike, even riding it for the first time. It felt so good! I can't stop thinking about it!"

"I am so happy for you!" Courtney quietly cheered.

"What do you mean, happy for me?" Kara sincerely asked.

"I mean, I am happy for you. You are falling in love," Courtney said.

"I am?" Kara spoke shyly, but happily, "it feels so good. What do I do now?"

"It depends, does he feel the same way about you?" Courtney asked, but realized Kara would likely not know the answer.

"How am I supposed to know that?" Kara blurted out.

"Well, judging from the way Jeff described you two today, I think he might. Maybe you could ask him over for a barbecue or something?" Courtney suggested.

"That sounds a little cheesy," Kara said.

You mean, cheeseburgerry," Courtney said and they both laughed.

"I guess it does sound cheesy," Courtney got up and gave Kara a big hug, "just think about it for a while. Between the two of us, I'm sure we can come up with a good plan."

"Thanks Courtney, I love you," Kara said as she hugged her Aunt.

"Love you too, Kara," Courtney said, and added, "Congratulations."

They both laughed again.

Kara went toward her room and Courtney went toward the kitchen when she heard a scream coming from Kara and she ran that way.

When she approached Kara's room, she could see her dancing, and singing happy songs to herself.

"What is it?" Courtney asked, "I thought that there was an emergency or something, like a spider or mouse."

"There is! The whole time we have been talking about Danger, there has been a text message on my phone from him that he sent right after practice. I don't even know how I missed it!" Kara said with glee.

"Oh my hell," Courtney said as she covered her mouth, "what does it say already?"

"He wants to take me out Friday night!" Kara said, almost in a scream.

They both screamed with joy and laughter, dancing in a circular fashion together as they held each other by both hands.

Chapter 26 - Coach's Meeting

The following Monday came so quickly. Kara had spent most of her time, except for sleep, swimming, and dirt bike training, on her new street bike. As she rode to the first day of swim practice, her mind was not on swimming, even though she was on schedule to be there 30 minutes early to meet with the coaching staff and the other student coach. No, to her delight, her mind was not on swimming; she was thinking about that boy who had been such a pain to her for so many years, until recently. She was thinking about Danger, reviewing their last couple of training sessions, and the time they had spent together that weekend. Their first date went amazing! He was so much fun and they talked and laughed the entire time. On Saturday, they just went riding together, without an agenda or a destination, and stopped in a grassy field and had a picnic. She was so happy. She was smiling without anyone around. Smiling so big that she thought her helmet might break right in two.

When she got to the school, she rode her bike up near the front of the parking area where there was designated motorcycle parking. When she did, she noticed something she had never noticed before; she noticed a couple other street bikes. She wondered if they were always there or if she was just noticing them now that she was using that space as well. She noticed one in particular; it was bigger and nicer than hers, not that it mattered to her, but she just thought to herself, "I wonder who rides that beautiful machine?" It was the time of day that only the swim team coaching staff would be there, which intrigued her even more.

After parking her bike, she went right into the pool area and headed toward the coaches office. She could see, from across the pool area, that there were already a few people there, but she did not recognize them all. As she approached, one of them, a boy, who looked like he was in college, turned and looked at her. When their eyes met, she thought she heard someone say to her, "Well hello, who are you?"

She turned to look behind her, to see who had said that, but nobody was there, so she passed it off as her imagination. Then she looked at that same boy again as she got closer to the office. He was still looking at her and this time she noticed more about him. "Wow!" She said under her breath, "He is built. He is obviously a swimmer. I wonder who he is?" She had looked away, feeling awkward that he was still looking at her as she approached.

When she opened the door, Coach Anderson stood up and said, "Kara, come on in, we were just talking about you."

Kara smiled and said playfully, "I hope it was good."

"Of course it was! You are our newest swimming sensation; we have nothing, but good to say about you," Coach said.

Kara responded, "Oh, thank you. I hope I don't let you down. You seem to have such high expectations."

"Don't you worry about that. We are a team and take everyone for the ability they have and the effort they put in. But let's not get into that right now; I think introductions are appropriate." Coach then turned to some of the other adults in the room and introduced the two assistant coaches she had not met before, and the one she knew from tryouts. Then he turned to the college looking boy and said, "I would like to also introduce you to someone you will be spending a lot of time with this year…"

Kara was not sure what he was talking about, she did not know who this boy was, or why the coach would say that, but as he did, the thought occurred to her that he might be the other student coach, since he was the only other person there that was even close to student looking age.

The coach continued, "This is the other student coach, Cru."

Cru then looked right into Kara's eyes, she felt like he was looking into her very soul and said, "Kara, it is very nice to meet you. I hear you can swim as fast as any swimmer coach has ever seen."

Kara didn't say anything for a few seconds. She was just looking into his eyes. His voice seemed to be coming from within him, and speaking directly to her heart. She mumbled a little as she said, "Uh, ya, uh, it's nice to meet you too," stumbling over her words, which was a very unfamiliar experience for Kara, "as for the swimming, I don't know about that, I just love to swim."

"Me too," smiled Cru, "the water feels like home to me."

Kara smiled back, "Me too. That's cool."

The coach interrupted them and said, "It looks like the two of you will get along just fine, so let's talk about practice. The team will be here soon."

The coaching staff spent the next 20 minutes or so talking about the upcoming year and how excited they were about the team and what they planned to do to best prepare the team for the swim meets. They agreed to meet together as a coaching team before practice every Monday morning.

After the short meeting, Kara and Cru went to opposite locker rooms to get their suits on for practice and shower down. When Kara came out of the locker room, she saw Cru swimming some laps. She had never seen anyone swim the way he did. He sliced through the water like a single water ski, but not as fast, of course. He was making it look so easy and so beautiful. She stopped and watched him go back-and-forth a few times, until her friend Julie came up behind her, without her noticing, and said, "whatcha looking at, Kara?"

Kara jumped slightly, "You totally scared me Jules."

Julie gave her a confused look, "Ya, so what are you looking at? Is that Cru? It looks like Cru."

"How do you know him?" Kara asked with interest.

"I don't. I have just heard some of the other girls on the team talk about him; how they love to watch him swim," Julie said as she made a swooning action with her hands fanning her face.

"What's so great about him, he's not even that cute?" Kara asked, but inside her, she could not help but feel something different than the words coming out her mouth. True, she thought, he wasn't the typical gorgeous guy, with a perfect face, that all the girls would usually fall for. Cru was different. He wasn't ugly, but he just had a simple, humble looking face, nothing that would stop a girl who passed him in the hall. As Kara thought about this, she also had a few other ideas going through her mind, like how he looked so deep into her eyes when he talked; how he is built so strong, with big shoulders, strong arms, defined upper back, and long, strong legs. His most defining feature, though, was very unique. He had a very strong, defined, and muscular lower back.

She shook her head, as to get the distracted thoughts from her mind as Julie said, "Ya, right, Kara, as if you can't tell." They both looked at each other with open mouths, and Julie continued, "You are just standing here, literally staring."

"I am not!" Kara insisted, then said, "Let's go get some laps in."

Later that day, on the way home from practice, she was thinking about the boy she met that morning. Her mind was deep in thought and she just went riding around for a while. She eventually arrived home and began fixing lunch when her phone alerted her to a text message.

It was Danger, "Hey, what are you doing for lunch?"

"Oh, my heck!" She thought to herself, "I totally forgot about Danger." She had told him she would come over to his house to have brunch after swim practice. She put her food back in the fridge and texted him back, "Sorry dude, I'm on my way."

It was only a 10 minute ride to Danger's house, on the other side of town, but she didn't remember any of it when she got there. She was so confused. So torn. Why were all the great feelings she had had for Danger just the day, even the morning before, all of a sudden seeming to be gone? Who was this Cru? She didn't even know him, but he was encapsulating her thoughts.

She reached her arm up to knock on the door when Danger opened it, "Hey Kara, how was swim practice?"

As soon as she saw and heard Danger speak, all of her feelings for him returned. She was happy. She was filled with the excitement she had all last weekend, and looked forward to more. But then, after they had lunch, her mind confusingly reverted to the thoughts she had been having about Cru, and as she did, she knew she needed to talk to her Grandma about what was troubling her mind…

Grandma Helen had always been there for Kara. Throughout her whole life, whenever she had questions about anything, anytime. Grandma Helen was the one that Kara learned most of life's important lessons from, especially when it came to the lessons about being a woman. Courtney was as well, of course, but this was something different. Kara knew that this was one of those times that she needed her Grandma's unique wisdom.

Chapter 27 - The Rising Tide

Using her cool new bluetooth helmet, Kara called Jeff on her way to her Grandparents house and told him that she might be late to training this afternoon.

"Is everything okay?" Jeff asked.

"Yes, there is just something that came up that I just have to talk to Grandma about," Kara said as she was riding.

"Okay, but you're okay, right?" Jeff sounded concerned.

"Yes, I'm fine. It's just silly girl stuff," Kara said with a little laugh in her voice.

"Oh, it sounds like a 'Danger-ous' conversation to me," Jeff teased.

Kara moaned a sigh, "Oh brother, Jeff, that was so corny. I will be there as soon as I can, you dork."

When she arrived, Kara went walking right into the house, like she always did at her grandparents home. Their home was always so inviting and she always felt loved there.

"We are in the back, honey, come on back," she heard her grandma yell gently from the backyard.

Kara went through the house to the back where both Helen and Robert were relaxing on their back porch, looking out at the bay. She walked to Helen and gave her a big hug, and then gave Robert a kiss on the cheek.

"How did you know it was me?" Kara asked her Grandma.

"I always know when it's you," Helen said as she smiled and winked at Robert, who grinned and winked back.

"We heard your fancy new bike pull into the drive," Robert said, "who else do we know that drives one of those loud bullet bike things you kids have nowadays?"

"Were you wearing your helmet?" Helen asked, looking at Kara with her head slightly bent down so she could look over the top of her glasses, but also smiling with love.

"Yes, Grammy, I always do," Kara answered.

"Good, it scares me so much having you tear around on that thing," said Grandma.

"Do you want an ice cream sandwich?" Robert asked; he always had something to offer Kara when she was there visiting.

"No thanks Grampy, I just came to talk to Grammy about something," Kara said, kindly, to her Grandpa.

"Oh. Girl talk," Robert whispered and said, "I will leave you ladies alone, I hear an ice cream sandwich calling my name anyway."

Robert got up and went into the house.

"Sweetheart," Helen asked with a loving tone, "what's got you troubled?"

"Oh, you know, I just wanted to talk to you about something," Kara said to her Grandma, trying to assure her it was important, but not tragic.

"Anything, honey; what do you want to talk about today? Is it that Danger boy again?" Grandma inquired, "Courtney told me about you two hanging out together more nowadays."

"She did!?" Kara exclaimed with embarrassment, "what did she say?"

"Oh, don't you worry, she didn't say that much. She just said the two of you were getting along really well and she thought you might like him," Grandma was smiling.

There was a pause, and Kara said, "Oh, Grammy, I don't know what to do. I don't know what all these wild feelings and thoughts I am having are about."

"You're going to have to tell me all about it honey," her Grandma said with compassion.

"Oh, Grammy," moaned Kara, "I don't even know where to start."

"Just start from the start, tell me everything you're feeling," said Helen, "You know I am always here for you. I am happy to listen to you talking all day long."

"Well, you know Danger?" Kara asked rhetorically, "I have been competing against him most all my life. He has always been such a pain in my butt and he drives me crazy with all his stupid boy things he does. He was always so high on himself, thinking he was king of the world or something."

"It sounds like you really like him," Helen said with a little laugh.

"No," Kara continued, "that is how he used to be. He is different now. Ever since you told me I needed to beat him in a race, and I did, we have started to get along and be friends."

"Well, that's good, right?" Helen asked.

"Ya, it is," Kara paused, obviously deep in thought, "then the other day I went and asked him to go for a ride with me on my new bike, and when he did, I all of a sudden felt something so different, it was so strange. I felt myself wanting to spend time with him. I felt myself thinking about him the rest of the day and into the next. In fact, until this morning, it seemed like I was thinking about him constantly."

"Till this morning, you say? What happened this morning, dear?" Grandma was listening intently.

"I met Cru," Kara answered as she looked down and folded her arms.

"Cru?" Helen questioned.

"He is the other student coach on the swim team," Kara explained.

"Oh," Helen leaned toward Kara in her chair, "and what do you want to tell me about this Cru boy?"

"Grammy, he has these eyes," Kara looked down to the ground again, feeling a sort of embarrassment.

"He has eyes?" Helen asked jokingly, then answered her own rhetoric, "of course he does, but what is special about his eyes?"

"I mean," Kara said, "he is not a super good looking guy like all the girls would fall for. He's not ugly or anything. He is strong and fit like a swimmer, but he doesn't seem to get noticed by all the girls like some hot guys do. The swim girls notice him, for sure, because he is such a good swimmer. But like, in the halls at school, I don't think he gets noticed much at all."

"What about the eyes you mentioned?" Helen persisted, but kindly.

Kara thought for a moment, "I don't know how to explain it, Grammy. He has these eyes that seem to look right into my soul. When he talks to me, even just a simple "hello", it's like he is speaking right to my heart, soul, and mind. It's like he doesn't even need to use words. I know that doesn't make any sense though."

Helen's eyes widened, but she said nothing.

"What's the matter, Grammy?" Kara asked.

"Oh, nothing," she said smiling and winking, "I was just listening to your beautiful description of this boy you like."

"I didn't say I like him!" Kara said emphatically.

"Okay, remember who you're talking to. I am your Grammy. I know you like nobody else knows you. It's okay that you like this boy," Helen paused, "and it's okay that you like Danger too."

Kara stood up and lifted her arms in the air, then down to her side, "But I don't know if I like him. And what about my feelings for Danger? I just found out I might like him too." There was a short pause while Helen let her gather her thoughts. "Grandma, how do you know when you are in love?" Kara sat down and looked out at the water in the bay, "There, I said it. I said the lovey dovey word. How do I know if I'm falling in love?"

Helen smiled sweetly at her granddaughter and responded slowly, "That is something that is a little different for everyone. Some people say they know right away, like what you are possibly saying about Cru. Other people say love has to grow on you before you know, like you describe your feelings changing about Danger." Then Helen reached over and grabbed Kara gently by the hand, saying, "Honey, falling in love is like the tides of the ocean. Sometimes they are increasing, sometimes they are decreasing; sometimes the tide is overwhelming and all consuming and other times it is barely noticeable. The tide has different effects on different things, different people, and different parts of the earth and landscape, but there is one thing that all people share in common about the tide; no one can control it or stop it. It comes whether you want it or not, whether you expect it or not. The tide, like love, cannot be controlled by any man, woman, company, or anything earthly. We all have one thing in common when it comes to love; It can't be forced and it can't be stopped. We have to recognize it for what it means to each of us individually and learn to identify when it comes and goes, and when it is the kind of love that will last the test of time and the trials of life." Helen stood up and lifted Kara up by the hand with her, pulling her into a hug. "Be patient, my dear, you will know when it is love and there will not be anything you can do about it."

Kara hugged her Grandma for a short while and asked, "How did you know when you loved Grandpa?"

Helen gently released Kara from their embrace and sat back down beside her. She smiled brightly and her eyes began to tear as she just smiled at Kara.

"Oh Grammy, that is so sweet!" Kara said softly, "you're still in love with Grampy, aren't you?"

Helen smiled ear to ear and said, "I love your grandpa more every day. He is the man of my dreams."

"How did you know it? I mean, the first time?" Kara politely persisted.

Helen began after a short pause to gather her thoughts and said reflectingly, "It was a day I will never forget. I was actually swimming in this very sea, a lot like you enjoy doing so much. It was a typical day, nothing special going on. I was just in the bay swimming with some of my friends when your grandfather came in from a fishing trip with his crew. He was standing at the helm, holding the wheel, like it was part of him. He looked like one of the mighty captains of heroic sea stories your dad and grandpa have undoubtedly told you about."

"Yes, they have," Kara said, "I love to hear those stories."

"Well," Grandma continued, "one of my friends said, "Helen, look," so I did, and when I looked, I saw your grandfather for the first time. Just like I described."

"That was it? You just saw him and fell in love?" Kara asked innocently.

Helen said, "Not so fast. Let me continue; When I looked at him, he turned and looked at me, as if he had felt me looking at him. He walked to the side of his boat and waved. I waved back. All my friends were embarrassed and swam away by then, but I just kept looking at him and he kept looking at me. Until, that is, one of his crew yelled his name, because the boat had drifted off course. He went back to steering and I went underwater. I swam to where he could not see me. I watched him for, oh, I don't know exactly how long… the rest of the day, maybe. There was something about him that just had my attention. I felt I was drawn to him, even though I didn't even know his name. I spent the next few days planning some way to meet him or see him again and when we finally met each other at the docks later that week, it was like we already knew each other. He asked me out and the rest is history."

"Wow Grammy!" Kara said, "you were in love the first time you saw Grampy?"

"I felt like I was, Kara, but it doesn't always work out like that. Like I said, it is different for everyone. But there is one thing most people in love will agree upon; you will know it when it happens." Helen paused, "And remember, falling in love is like the tide; you can't force it and you can't control it, but it will overwhelm you when it gets hold of you. And there's nothing you can do to stop the ocean tide OR true love."

Chapter 28 - The Plan

A few weeks later, and just a couple days before the first swim meet of the season, Kara was talking to Julie.

"So what are you going to do about the two boy problem?'" Julie asked.

"Oh, Jules, I don't know. What do you think I should do?" Kara asked with a sigh.

"Have they met each other?" Julie asked, "Does Danger know you have another crush?"

"No way!" Kara exclaimed, "Could you imagine if they were friends or something? That would totally suck."

"So seriously, Kara," Julie asked again, "what are you going to do?"

"Why can't I like both of them?" Kara said with a grin, "What's the harm in that?"

"Nothing, at first," Julie answered, "but then you start falling for them more and more. Then you start thinking you can get away with having two boyfriends. Then, when you least expect it, they find out about each other, and you lose both of them."

Julie was making an explosion gesture with her hands over her head.

"That's not going to happen," Kara reached over and gave Julie a friendly push.

"It could though." They both laughed and Julie said once more, "So, seriously this time, what are you going to do about the two boy problem?"

Kara put her finger up to her head in a playful manner, as if to show that she was deep in thought, with a smirk on her face, "Ah ha!" She exclaimed, "Maybe they SHOULD meet!?"

"What!?" Julie shouted, then a little quieter, said, "are you crazy or something?"

They both grabbed each other laughing.

Kara said, "No, I'm serious, maybe they should meet. In fact, maybe if I see them together, I will get a better idea of what I should do about my two boy problem you are so concerned about."

"Actually, that might work," Julie put her arm around Kara and put her head on her head, "what then, little Miss smarty-pants, do you have in mind to get them to meet?"

"I was going to invite Danger to the swim meet Friday anyway, I'm sure we can think of some way to have them run into each other." They both giggled and grabbed each other's hands.

"This is going to be so much fun!" Julie said with excitement.

Later that day, after training, Kara was talking to Danger, "So, do you have any major plans this weekend?" He asked her.

"Nothing major," Kara responded slowly, "why?"

"I was thinking we should go out," said Danger.

"Oh, you were thinking, huh?" Kara said teasingly, "what exactly do you have in mind?"

Danger responded, "I know we do a lot of riding together on the trails around town, here at the track, and at races, but I was thinking you might like to take a trip with me on Saturday and explore some of the riding trails around Laredo. What do you think?"

"That sounds really fun! But," Kara hesitated.

"But what?" said Danger.

Kara reached toward him and gave him a playful poke in the chest, "Only if you do something for me first."

With an odd look on his face, Danger said, "Okay, what is it?"

"Friday night I have a swim meet and I want you to come," Kara said, poking him lightly in the chest again.

"Of course I'll come!" Danger said excitedly, "I would love to come!"

"Good. It starts at six, but I probably won't swim until about a quarter after, so you have some leeway to be a little late if you don't mind sitting wherever there might be a seat left. It can get crowded at times." Kara looked down, thought about what she and Julie had talked about, wondering if it still was the right thing to do. She then looked at Danger, right into his eyes, as if in hopes of seeing and feeling what she does when Cru talks to her, but she did not.

"What?" Danger asked.

"Oh, nothing," Kara gave him a hug and said, "I am glad you're coming."

"I'm excited to come and see you swim competitively," Danger said softly. "Then we will hit the road about six in the morning Saturday, okay?"

"Okay, see you tomorrow," Kara began to push her bike back to the garage, still thinking about her plan, then she turned back and said, "just wait for me out by our bikes after the meet Friday night."

After she got home that evening, Kara texted Julie, "Hey you."

"Don't hate me," she texted back, "Did you ask Danger to the meet?"

Kara replied, "Yes, I did." She added a scared face emoji.

"What's wrong, girlfriend?" Julie asked.

"I'm still just wondering if it is the right thing to do," Kara texted with a confused face emoji as she audibly let out a little groan to herself, "I don't want to cause any trouble or anything. They are both such awesome guys."

The text bubbles showed on Kara's phone as she waited for Julie's reply, which said, "Oh, Kara, don't worry so much. It's going to be fine. Plus, you don't even know if they are actually going to meet, lol."

"I guess you're right," Kara typed out, "I should just let it play out however it's going to happen."

Julie's response came quickly and had some spelling and grammar errors, like she had voice texted it, "Of course I'm right! I'm coming over, let's make some pre-meet spaghetti and talk about the big plan."

"Awesome! See you in a few," Kara closed her phone and changed into some sweat pants and hoodie.

Chapter 29 - They Meet at the Meet

"Would you look at that kid swim!" The district swim meet announcer said to the stat recorder next to him, "He looks like a freakin' motorboat!"

"That's Cru," the girl said to him, "have you never seen him swim before?"

"Yes, I have," he responded, "but it amazes me like the first time, every time I see him swim; the kid is awesome!"

"Have you ever seen Kara swim?" She asked.

"No, who is Kara?" he said.

"Kara is the new freshman swimmer Cru's team got this year. They say she can swim just as fast as Cru," she said clearly.

"Who said that?" The announcer looked shocked, "a girl who can swim as fast as that motorboat out there?"

"That's what they say," the stat keeper explained, "My friend told me that none of the other girls even come close to her when they race. She is like twice as fast as them or something."

"Well I see, sounds intriguing. Where is this Kara?" he asked.

"She races four or five of the events, so she should be in the next race," she looked around and then pointed to the far side of the pool, "over there. There she is."

The announcer looked and said, "That girl with the super blonde hair? She can swim as fast as Cru?"

"That's what they say," she said.

"Which event is next for her?" he asked.

"The 200 meter freestyle," she said after verifying with her program sheets.

"Okay," he said, "I am looking forward to seeing this."

Meanwhile, Kara and Julie were doing some dynamic stretching and warm ups near the pool, getting ready for the race to begin.

"So, are you still going to do it?" Julie asked, "Is Danger here?"

"Yes, he is here," Kara said, as she pointed him out across the pool and waved.

"Oh, he is sooo cute!" Julie said, smiling and bumping her hip into Kara.

"I know, right?" Kara smiled and continued, "and yes, I am still going forward with the plan. I feel better about it today."

"Good! I think it is a good idea. Now let's swim!" Julie said, then added, "Kara, please don't hold back this time. I know how fast you can swim. Just go out and swim like you and I both know you can. Don't feel like you have to slow down to let the rest of us feel better. Just kick our butts. It's okay, I promise."

"Oh Jules, you're so nice," Kara said, "I am not that fast."

"Kara, you listen to me right now," Julie was speaking very sternly, but in a calm and playful manner, "you are the fastest swimmer I've ever seen, at any level. There is nothing wrong with that. Just go out and swim! Swim like you are in the ocean that you love so much and talk about all the time. This is freestyle and you can swim like a fish, so just go do it!"

Kara shrugged and said, "Thanks girlfriend, we'll see how I feel when the water hits me."

The two girls hugged and went to their blocks. Kara looked over at Julie a few seconds before the gun sounded. Julie smiled and winked, mouthing the words, "Swim girl, swim."

The next sound heard, after the gun, was the announcer, saying, "It looks like Julie in lane five has started off in the lead, with Amy in lane seven, second, and…" Then he stopped and turned to the stat keeper, "Where is Kara?"

She looked up and stood up from her chair to get a better look, pointing at the pool about the 25 meter mark, or half of the pool length; "There she is, she is still under the water."

"What? What do you mean?" The announcer stood up from his chair to see what was being described. Dumbfounded, he said, "How is she so far ahead when she has not even surfaced yet? That doesn't make any sense. Who swims like that?"

As Kara surfaced, nearly three quarters of the way down the pool, she was 10 meters ahead of the other swimmers. The announcer went back to his microphone, "A correction folks, it looks like Kara, in lane three, is in the lead." He then turned to the stat girl again, and said, "How did she do that? I have never, in all my years of watching competitive swimming, seen anyone swim so fast underwater. She looked like she could've gone the whole length of the pool."

"I don't know," she responded while opening her hands up in a small shrug, "I told you, they said she was fast, but I have never seen her myself."

"Wow," The announcer chuckled and sat back down and said again, "wow, just wow, look at her go."

As the race completed, Kara was a full pool length ahead of Julie, who eventually took second place. When she completed the race, she simply got out of the pool, sat on the edge, and looked to see some of the other swimmers making their final turn. She then looked around the stadium at the fans. Everyone was looking at her, not clapping and cheering, just silently looking at her. She did not understand what was going on, and felt very alone and awkward.

Within seconds, she instinctively put that feeling aside and turned to the pool. She got up and walked to lane five and yelled, "Go Julie, go!"

With that action, the fans in the stadium began to slowly cheer again, then, louder, until it sounded like it should in the final meters of a swimming race, very loud and indistinguishable.

Julie finished the race in second place, turning to look at the results board to see her placement and time. Then she immediately looked at Kara and said, "Holy crap, Kara, you really did swim. You are in a different league than the rest of us. Good job girl!"

"Thanks, Jules," Kara offered her a high five hug, "You swam awesome too!"

Their coach then approached them and said to Kara, "You know, I have been the swim coach for over 20 years at this school. I have taken teams to state and come back with the title. I have even sent swimmers to the nationals, but I have never, in all my life, seen anything like I just saw."

"Really?" Kara said to her coach.

"Kara, that was amazing," she heard Cru say as he walked up from behind her.

Kara turned around and immediately saw Cru's eyes looking right into her like she loved so much. "Thanks Cru," she said, "you did awesome too. Was anyone even close to you today?"

"Sure they were. It was a good race," he said, even though they both knew he was just being modest. It wasn't close in his race either.

Cru turned to walk away, not wanting to intrude on her conversation with Julie when Kara said, "Hey Cru, Jules and I are going out to get something to eat after, do you want to come?" She paused and added, "Full disclosure, my friend Danger is joining us too. Do you know Danger?"

"Hell yes, I'd love to come! But no, I don't know Danger," He said with a cheesy grin, "What do you have in mind?"

"I don't know exactly," Kara said to him, "just meet us outside the locker room after the last race."

"Cool," said Cru, as he gave them a hang loose gesture and walked away.

When all the races were completed and Kara and Julie had showered and cleaned up, they were walking out toward the hallway when Kara thought she heard Cru talking to her, "Thanks for asking me to go with you guys," she thought she heard him say. She turned to see if he was behind her, but he was not. As they walked out of the locker room, there he was waiting for them.

"Thanks for asking me to go with you guys," said Cru.

"Did you just say that a few seconds ago?" asked Kara with a bewildered look of confusion on her face. As soon as the words left her mouth, she realized how silly it might sound.

"Say what?" Cru asked, just as confused.

"Did you just... Oh, never mind," Kara passed it off again, deciding it was her imagination and didn't want to sound stupid. She changed the question, "Did you ride your bike tonight?"

"Ya. You too?" he asked.

"Of course!," Kara said, "It beats that old truck my uncle lets me drive."

"What are you driving, Julie?" Cru asked.

"Nothing," Julie said as she leaned into him as they were talking, "I was dropped off. Can I ride with you?"

"Sure," Cru said, then he looked at Kara and asked, "Is that alright with you?"

Kara looked surprised that he asked and simply said, "Of course, I don't care." Then she added, "Just drive safe. That's my bestie you got there."

The three of them began to walk out to the parking lot. As they left the building, Kara could see Danger standing by their bikes, just like she asked him to. She turned to look at Julie and gave her a pretend scared look, which was matched by Julie.

As they approached, Danger took his earbuds out of his ears and said, "Hey."

"What's up, Danger boy?" Julie said with a little wit.

"Funny," he said.

"Danger, this is our friend, Cru," Kara said quietly, then turned to Cru and added, "Cru, this is my friend, Danger."

Danger extended his fist for a bump, "What's up?"

Cru gave him a fist bump and asked, "Your name is Danger?"

"Your name is Cru?" Danger had heard that question his whole life and was sometimes annoyed by it. This time, he decided to answer by asking the same question in return.

"Sorry man," Cru said, "Cool, Is this your bike?" Cru gestured to the bike Danger was leaning on.

Danger had ridden one of his biggest, most powerful dirt bikes that day, which he had modified to be street legal.

"Ya, it is," he responded.

"Sweet," Cru said, "where do you do most of your riding?"

"I'm a dirt track rider, mostly in motocross and supercross events, but lately I have been getting out and hitting some trails. I think it would be cool to start doing some motorcycle rally racing," Danger explained.

"What?" Kara said, as she had never heard him mention that.

"That does sound fun, I mostly ride streets, but I have always been interested in getting out on a little dirt," Cru said.

Meanwhile, Kara and Julie were looking at each other in amazement at how well the two of them were getting along and how neither of them seemed to care that they were both interested in Kara, or even if they had any idea that was the situation with them.

"We should all go out to the hills sometime," Danger suggested, "we have enough bikes for everyone, if needed."

"Cool, let's do it sometime," said Cru.

"Jules, you in?" Kara said to Julie with the thought that she would probably decline.

"I guess so, but I have never ridden a motorcycle before," Julie said, fully knowing one of the two boys would offer to teach her.

She was right: Both boys, wanting to impress Kara with their willingness to help her friend, said at the same time, practically in unison, "I will teach you."

They looked at each other, about to say more, but Kara interrupted, "I, I will teach her boys, she will do better if I help her."

"No, it's okay, Kara," Julie said smiling, "the boys can take turns teaching me. And then you can fix what I am doing wrong, if so." She released a flirty laugh as she reached out with both arms and touched both the boys shoulders.

They all laughed. Then as they all got on the bikes, Kara said, "follow me. Keep up, if you can."

Later that night, when Kara was dropping her off at her home, Julie asked, "So what are you going to do now that the two boys meeting each other didn't help anything? Can you believe how well they got along?"

Kara sighed, "I know. I can't believe they are actually going to go riding together. That was definitely not my plan. I was hoping one of them would be a big jerk to the other or something."

Julie shrugged and said, "I guess they just have no clue that they both like you."

"I haven't told them, of course, and neither of them have seen me with the other, so I suppose they have no reason to know," Kara said sadly.

"What now?" Julie asked.

"Back to plan A, I guess," Kara said jovially, "I date both of them until something or someone tells me that one is more right for me than the other."

"What else is a girl to do?" Julie paused and then said, with a big grin on her face, "Well, I guess you could give one of them to me. You know I'd do that for you."

"Oh, I totally would, if that were possible. I love you more than both of them, you're my very best friend." Then Kara added, "Just know, if one of them does ask you out, it's no big deal to me. I would be totally happy for you!"

"I know, silly, I was just kidding," Julie hugged Kara, "and I don't think that will happen."

"If it does, it does," Kara said, "see you later then?"

"See you later girl," Julie turned and walked into her house.

Chapter 30 - The Cave

"Nice win today, Kara," Cru said after a swim meet near the end of the season.

"Thanks Cru, you too," Kara replied, "you swept all your races, didn't you? I wasn't really paying attention, but figured you did."

"Just like you did, smarty-pants," Cru said playfully.

Kara said, "I really love that I decided to join the team. I have always loved swimming, especially in the ocean water, but it never even occurred to me that swimming competitively would be so much fun!"

"I couldn't agree more," Cru said, smiling.

As Kara was about to head into the locker room, Cru got her attention and asked, "Hey, do you want to come over to my house tomorrow night? My parents really want to have you over for dinner."

"Oh, shoot, I can't. I have plans tomorrow night," Kara said, noticing the disappointment on Cru's face, "but I'd be happy to crash their party tonight, if that works?"

"Okay, cool," Cru said quickly, "let me text them and find out. I'll see you in a few."

They both went their separate ways and Cru worked it out with his parents to have Kara come over that evening.

"I don't see anything here," Kara said on the phone with Cru, as she was pulled over on the side of the road where Cru had explained to her where he lived.

"Where are you?" He asked.

"Right where you said to go," Kara said, "and all I see is a big garage."

"Yep, that's it," Cru confirmed.

"You live in a garage?" asked Kara.

"No, of course not," Cru said.

"Then what do you mean, that's it?" Kara said, wondering.

"I will meet you there in about thirty seconds and open the door for you," Cru said as he hung up the phone, saying, "see you in a sec."

Kara was not counting, but about 20 seconds later, one of the three garage doors began to open. When it was up, there stood Cru, yelling down the driveway for her to "come on in."

Kara rode her bike up the driveway and into the garage next to Cru.

"What took you so long?" Cru joked.

"What took YOU so long?" Kara replied, knowing he was joking.

As the door closed behind them, Kara started looking around and inquired, "Why isn't there a house with your garage?"

Cru answered, "It's all underneath."

"Underneath?" Kara asked with a confused tone.

"You'll see," Cru said, like it was routine.

Then the door closed completely and Cru said, "Have you ever been to that amusement park, the one with the room that lowers down and it looks like the walls are getting taller?"

"Yes, I love it!" Kara answered.

"Well, don't be surprised then," Cru said.

When Cru said that, he led her to a small adjacent room, walked over to the wall and pushed a button. Then the floor began to drop, like a massive elevator and Cru walked back to Kara and took her hand.

"What is going on?" Kara asked, looking around with curiosity.

"We are going inside," Cru said matter-of-factly.

"You live under the ground?" Kara asked, still in wonder.

"Mostly," Cru said.

"What do you mean, mostly?" Kara continued to inquire what was going on.

"You'll see," Cru said, looking up and the ceiling getting farther away.

"Oh, great, another "you'll see," Kara laughed briefly, "Why don't you just tell me?"

"Cause it is more fun to show you," Cru said.

"Like I'm a guinea pig or a test rat?" Kara said, squeezing Cru's hand.

"No. I just love to see your beautiful eyes light up when you see something that surprises you; and I am pretty sure this will surprise you." Cru had moved closer to Kara and moved his arm up to her back, resting lightly between her shoulder blades.

As they reached the bottom of the descent, Kara did not know how far they had dropped. Suddenly, the whole wall in front of her opened up into a huge room of a house, like a large family room. There was a man and a woman, Cru's parents, standing there to greet them.

"Kara!" Cru's mother said, with her arms extended for a hug, "it is so nice to have you in our home, please come in."

"Hi, Mrs. Requin, thank you," Kara said politely.

"Please, call me Sierra. Would you like something to drink before dinner? We have a soda machine," she said.

Kara replied, "Sure, but I will just have some water, thank you."

"Can I show you around or did Cru say he would?" Sierra offered.

"I will, Mom," Cru interjected.

For the next 15 minutes, Cru gave Kara a tour of his family's home.

"What does your dad do for work again?" Kara asked while they were walking.

"He is a Captain in the United States Coast Guard," Cru answered proudly.

"Really?" Kara said, "That's awesome! That kinda explains why you are such a good swimmer."

"I guess it doesn't hurt my chances, having a dad who is always in the water. He has taught me a lot," Cru said.

"Ya, me too. I guess that makes sense for both of us with Dad's around the water all the time," Kara agreed.

"My family is through and through Coast Guard," Cru explained, "my father, my grandpa, my uncles, even some of our aunts. My mom is Coast Guard reserve, but as much as she goes out, she might as well be full-time and enlisted. She loves just going out anytime my Dad gets the call."

Kara said, "That is so cool!"

"We love it; there is nothing better than being able to help someone out at sea, who has run into trouble that they were not expecting. Even the navy needs us sometimes," Cru said, obviously very proud of his family and the work they do.

"Hey, are you kids ready to eat?" Cru's mom called from the kitchen.

"Yes, mom, we will be right there," Cru answered.

"But you haven't surprised me with anything yet," Kara said inquisitively and sarcastically because she was well enough surprised to see a huge home at the bottom of a garage elevator. Cru had told her that that was not the coolest part of the surprise.

"I guess it'll have to wait until after dinner," Cru said.

"Oh, come on, just show me now," Kara pleaded.

Cru let out a, "Hmmmm," then continued, "No, we need more time. I will show you after dinner."

Kara enjoyed dinner with Cru and his family, which was made up of his father, mother, an older brother, and a younger sister.

"You have such an awesome family, Cru," Kara said after dinner.

"Thanks. When do I get to meet all your family?" asked Cru.

"My family? I will have to see when my dad, uncle, and aunt are all going to be in the same place, and let you know," Kara responded.

"It's a date then?" Cru said, happily and playfully.

"It's a date!" Kara confirmed with a smile, "Now what else do you have to show me?"

"Close your eyes and take my hand," Cru spoke softly.

"Is this just a trick to hold my hand?" Kara joked, "you know you can hold it anytime you want."

"Kinda, but just do it anyway," They both laughed as Kara closed her eyes and took Cru's hand.

She could hear him talk to her as he led her through the home and down some stairs. She felt so good inside. She loved that she was able to see him in her mind as he talked to her, feeling his simple words in her heart.

"Is this how love feels?" She thought to herself.

"Okay, we are almost there," Cru let go of her hand and put his arm on her shoulders to guide her every step until he brought them to a stop, and he walked around in front of her.

"Open your eyes," he said.

Kara did and the first thing she saw was Cru standing in front of her looking into her eyes. Then she looked around him and saw what looked like a cave with two large, thick glass doors at the end in the direction she was facing. They appeared to be holding back water.

"What is this?" Kara said in awe.

"It is, for lack of a better explanation, a secret passage to the ocean," Cru said.

"Seriously? A secret passage?" Kara released a sarcastic laugh, but still asked sincerely, "How does it work?"

Cru explained, "There are some controls by the doors that release and drain all the water in those two rooms so we can open them and go inside. Once inside and ready to swim, there is another control valve that fills the room back up with water, then opens the door on the other side, allowing us to swim out, directly into the bay."

"How far down are we?" Kara asked.

"Not as far as it seems; about 50 feet," Cru answered.

"Isn't the water pressure too much for you to just swim away?" Kara inquired.

Cru gave her a strange look, paused, then said, "Ya, of course it is. We get our scuba gear on first."

"Oh, that makes more sense," Kara said.

"Do you want to try it with me sometime?" Cru invited.

Kara responded, "I'd love to, but I'm embarrassed to say that, even though I have been swimming my whole life, I have never actually gone scuba diving, at least with equipment that is."

"It's a date then?" Cru said with vigor and a smile.

"It's a date!" Kara smiled, "do you have any other ideas to get dates out of me today?"

Cru paused, smiled, and put his left hand on Kara's waist. "I want to go out with you anytime I can."

Kara put her arms up on his shoulders, "Okay, then just ask anytime."

They both drew each other into a hug. Cru swayed back and forth and began to hum a little tune like they were dancing.

"I feel really good with you," Kara said.

"Me too," Cru whispered, "this feels right to me."

He leaned down to give her a their first kiss, but she turned her head and said, "Not tonight Cru, I want to take a little more time getting to know you."

After a short pause, Cru said, "Okay, it's a date then," and kissed her on the forehead.

They both laughed and hugged for a few more moments before they released and smiled at each other for a while longer, until Kara said, "I should probably go now."

Chapter 31 - Dangerous Encounter

"Hey, glad you could make it," Danger said sarcastically when Kara showed up thirty minutes late for the day trip they had planned, to go riding in the hills upstate.

Sorry, I don't usually sleep through my alarm like that, but it had been going off for almost an hour by the time it woke me," Kara said, a little irritated.

Kara had been up very late the night before, talking to her Grandma about Cru and her feelings for him. Then when she got home, she went through all the same questions and conversations about feelings with Courtney. Kara was so glad to have two such wonderful women in her life who were always there to help her in any way they could with the things involving growing into womanhood. When she did finally go to bed, she could not sleep. She tossed and turned, tossed and turned; she still could not decide, even after talking so long with her Grandma and Aunt, if she did the right thing by not kissing Cru. She wondered if he still liked her. She wondered if he was mad at her. She wondered if he would even talk to her again. And then there was Danger; what about him? What about her feelings for him? How was she supposed to sleep with all this going on in her mind? To her best guess, she eventually fell asleep about three in the morning.

"Did you hear anything I just said?" Asked Danger, about 15 minutes into their drive.

"What?" responded Kara, who was in and out of sleep, dozing off in the passenger seat.

"I was just telling you about where we are going today and you totally ignored me. It's like you're in a daydream or something," Danger said kindly.

"I did?" Kara said.

"Ya, what's going on?" Danger reached over and put his hand on Kara's knee.

"I just didn't sleep very well, I'm sorry," Kara replied.

"Don't worry about it," he tickled her leg a little bit and she smiled and put her hand on his, then he asked "are you okay to go riding today?"

Kara perked up, "Of course! I have been looking forward to it."

Kara then looked down at his hand on her leg and the way he caressed her. She did care for him, she truly did, and she felt a distinct romantic connection with her hand on his. She had had such strong feelings for Danger before. She was searching her soul to find the feelings she once felt, to see if they were as strong, but she just wasn't feeling it like she hoped. Her mind was a storm of thoughts and confusion.

"Well," Danger asked, "is it?"

Kara looked at him and asked in reply, "Is it what?"

"I said, is it bothering you for me to have my hand on your leg?" Danger sounded a bit disturbed, but still spoke kindly "you were just staring down at it like it's bothering you."

Kara turned her body in her seat, bringing her left leg up on the seat and tucked it underneath her right leg so that she was facing Danger as he drove the truck. As she did, Danger pulled his hand away. She then reached over, grabbed his hand gently, and put it back on her leg. She put her other hand on Dangers hand as well, "no, it is not bothering me. I like it, I just have so much on my mind right now."

"Well, the good news is that we have another hour or so to drive," Danger said, "why don't you tell me about what's on your mind."

"Oh Danger, that is so sweet, but it is so much mushy girl stuff, I'm sure I would bore you to death," she said.

Danger looked away from the road briefly and said to her, "You won't know if you don't try telling me."

Kara hesitated before she replied, "I know, but I would rather just talk to you about something else, is that okay?"

"I guess so," Danger said.

There was a long silence. They both had a lot on their mind about their feelings for each other, but neither of them wanted to talk about it.

"So how is your new jump coming?" Kara broke the silence with a question, "What are you going to call it?"

Kara knew Danger would want to talk about his jumping. She had seen him working so hard lately on a new jump involving laying the bike horizontal while turning it around twice in the air before leveling out the bike and landing. It was the hardest jump she had ever seen or heard of in her career and experiences with Supercross or freestyle jumping.

"It's getting there," Danger said quietly, "I am almost ready to start jumping it on one of the launch ramps and airbag landing, instead of the foam pit."

"Awesome," Kara said excitedly, "What are you going to call it?"

Danger paused a few seconds before saying, "I don't know, maybe something like table top?"

"BORE-ING!" Kara said with a moan and emphasis.

Danger looked at her with a smirk and said, "Well, little miss critique, do you have a better idea for a name?"

Kara laughed and made a deep in thought type gesture before she said, "Since you invented it and are going to be the first one to do anything like it, you should use your name in the name of the jump."

"Do you think so?" Danger asked.

"Totally," Kara said, "You can call it something like Danger's double dare."

"Hmmm, I kinda like it," Danger put his hand to his chin, mimicking the gesture Kara had made, and said, "Danger's double dare; it has a nice ring to it."

"I can't wait to see you land it on the live ramps!" Kara said as she squeezed his hand.

"Thanks, Care Bear," he said, using a nickname that he occasionally called Kara. She didn't care for it much, but allowed him to use it. She grinned.

Both Kara and Danger looked out their own windows for a few minutes, as they contemplated their own thoughts. It was only a few more minutes until they arrived at the area they were going to park the truck and hit the trails with their bikes.

"It's beautiful up here," Kara said, looking around the hills that surrounded them like walls of a giant maze.

"You're beautiful," Danger said with a grin.

Kara playfully punched him in the chest, "Don't be cheesy."

"I'm serious, you are. I have always thought so," Danger said as he put his arm around her shoulder in a side hug.

"Oh, that's sweet of you," Kara said softly. "Thanks Danger boy."

"I don't like that," Danger said somewhat abruptly.

"Why not, Danger boy?" She said playfully.

"Please don't call me that," Danger said, "I'm not a little kid."

"I know you're not," Kara said as she reached toward him to tickle him, "you're a big, sexy man, but you'll always be Danger boy to me."

Danger playfully growled and sneered.

"Oh, come on, I love Danger boy," Kara kick-started her bike and said, "race you to that field up there."

"What field?" Danger said as Kara spun her wheel and took off.

Danger quickly started his bike and the chase was on. They spent the next few hours riding the trails and trying to explore new paths through the hills. They found a few steep hills and challenged each other to climb them. They found some natural jumps and competed to see who could jump the farthest. Kara was feeling very good and having a lot of fun with Danger when they came back to the truck for some lunch.

They folded down the tailgate of the truck and got the food from the cooler. He had prepared Kara's favorite sandwich, Monte Cristo, which was usually best eaten warm, so he had even packed a little hot plate he could plug into the truck and warm it up.

Kara saw what he was doing and said, "Oh my Helena Montana, you did not!? I can't believe you made me a Monte Cristo, you are so sweet!"

"Sweet again?" Danger rolled his eyes, "Sweet? Like my grandma calls me sweet?"

Kara giggled and said, "Oh, come on, Danger boy. You ARE sweet. It's okay to be sweet. I like sweet!"

Danger looked away, as if he was put off, or maybe embarrassed.

"What's wrong?" She inquired, "are you mad that I called you Danger boy? Or are you mad that I think you're sweet?"

"I am not mad," he said.

"What then?" Kara asked.

He didn't answer.

Kara asked again, "Come on D, what is it?"

After a few moments, Danger responded, "I don't want to be your sweet guy friend."

"What do you mean you don't want to be my sweet guy friend?" Kara asked, even though she felt she knew what he meant.

Danger turned and stepped back from the truck some, and said, "I mean, I don't want to be your friend who is just a nice guy to hang around with."

Kara said sweetly, "But you are my friend and you are nice and you are fun to hang around with."

"I know," Danger uncharacteristically stumbled on his words as he stepped back to the truck and sat down near her, "I mean, you are too, but…"

Kara, purely out of instinct, moved closer to him, so they were sitting side-by-side and took his hand, and said, "but what, Danger?"

There was a long silence. Then Danger turned to Kara and looked her right in the eyes, taking her by the other hand, and said, "Kara, I like you. I really like you. I have liked you for a long time. I have liked you since we were little kids."

Danger stopped talking to let Kara respond, but she said nothing; both of them just looked into each other's eyes, smiling.

After just a few seconds, Danger nervously broke the silence and began to say, "Don't you have anything to…"

But before he could finish his sentence, Kara reached up to his chest, grabbing his shirt in her hand and pulling him toward her. Their lips met softly, and they kissed, both of them closing their eyes, and feeling the moment neither of them expected to have that day. The kiss lasted a few seconds.

Kara let go of Danger, and they moved apart from the kiss, opening their eyes and looking at each other once more. Both of them were smiling.

"That was…" Kara began to say, but stopped. She did not know what she was feeling. She did not know why she kissed Danger, when just a couple days before, she wanted so much to have kissed Cru, but she did not let him.

"That was nice and," she continued slowly, "comfortable."

"Well, that's not what I hoped to hear after a kiss," Danger said with a somewhat sad look, and feeling a little confused.

"Ya. No. I mean…" Kara was now stumbling on her words, "I know. I don't mean comfortable."

"What then?" Danger asked.

"I don't know!" Kara said quickly, but softly so Danger would know she's not mad or anything.

Danger said, "Because you kissed me… I mean, I kissed you too, but I wasn't exactly expecting that today."

"Dammit Danger," Kara said as she put her hand on his leg and squeezed, "I am so confused."

"About what?" Danger asked, "About kissing me?"

"About everything… About you… About Cru," Kara covered her mouth with her hand, realizing that she had just said something that she didn't really want to.

"Cru?" Danger said as he removed his arm from around Kara.

"Uggghh," Kara clenched her fists, "why is this so hard?"

"What about Cru?" Danger asked as he folded his arms and leaned back toward the side of the truck bed.

Kara waited a few moments before she responded, "Cru and I have been seeing each other for a few months now and we are having a really good time. I think I really like him."

"Oh, okay. So we haven't been seeing each other too, for a few months, or longer?" Asked Danger, very confused, and fighting feelings of hurt.

"I know, I know. That's why I am so confused," Kara said, "You are such a good and amazing friend.. and I know that is not what you want to be, but I just don't know what I want right now."

"A good friend?" Danger said, "Ouch, that hurts."

"Oh Danger, don't take it like that," Kara pleaded as she reached for his hand, "You are a good friend and I love spending time with you. I love the things we have in common and I love that I can talk to you so easily. The time that we spend together means so much to me. Please don't take this the wrong way, I am just so confused."

"But we are just friends?" Danger gave her hand a little squeeze, "We just kissed. You just kissed me."

Kara looked down and said, "I know, but that is kind of what I'm trying to say. Did it feel right to you?"

Danger answered quickly, "My heart was racing faster than my bike on race day."

They both laughed softly and smiled.

"So was mine," Kara admitted, "but did it feel right?"

"What do you mean by right?" Danger looked confused still, and said "it didn't feel wrong. Did it feel wrong to you or something? Your first response was "comfortable," is that what you mean?"

"No, I don't think it was wrong either, but what I meant is that it just felt a little comfortable, like I said, like it was not romantic." Kara released a sigh and a grunt combination before continuing, "I know that might sound silly to you, but that is what I was feeling and I can't help that."

Danger looked in her eyes again and said, "So what, exactly, are you trying to say? Do you wish you had not kissed me?"

"No, no, no. I am glad I did, very glad, but it was not how I imagined my first…" Kara stopped talking and looked down.

"Kara," Danger lifted her chin gently, and took her by both hands, "it was my first kiss too, and I couldn't imagine anyone else in this world that I would've rather had it with."

Chapter 32 - It's All So Clear Now

"How was your day-date with Danger Saturday?" Asked Courtney, while Kara was having some french toast Jeff had made them for breakfast.

"It was so good!" Kara said happily.

"So good?" Courtney echoed Kara's happiness, "You are definitely going to have to give me the deets when you respond with an answer like that."

Courtney sat down by Kara, who was smiling brighter than the sun.

Kara finished chewing and said, "I think I have figured it out."

Courtney asked, "Figured it out? You mean, which of the two boys you like more?"

"Even better," Kara put down her fork, "I think I have figured out what falling in love feels like."

"Kara Danielle Landers, you better not be kidding me right now!" Courtney said emphatically.

Kara said playfully, "I'm not, I'm serious. I think I'm in love."

"Oh girl, you tell me everything right now. I am totally calling the school and telling them you are not coming in today," Courtney insisted kindly.

"Courtney, you are so cool," Kara said, "but I can't miss swim practice this morning."

"Okay, okay, I know," Courtney agreed, "then just give me a little bit of the details for now and I will talk to you more about it tonight."

Kara began eating her breakfast quicker and looked away from Courtney.

"What are you doing?" Courtney asked her.

"Eating," Kara said.

"Aren't you even going to give me one detail?" Courtney said with a little whine.

Kara kept eating until she was on the last bite, then said, "Just one for now and then I will talk to you later."

Kara got up, rinsed her plate in the sink and went to the bathroom to brush her teeth.

"Hello?" Courtney had followed her and knocked on the bathroom door, "I am waiting for my juicy nugget of information Kara."

Kara opened the door, walked swiftly past Courtney, and on her way out the door into the garage, turned and yelled with glee, "I kissed Danger!"

"Whaaaaat!?" Courtney screeched, then said loudly and happily, "You kissed Danger and you are leaving for school, leaving me hanging? You little stinker!"

Later that day, at school, Kara played a similar charade with Julie, but she did not have anywhere to run to after she told her about the kiss.

"So you do like Danger then?" Julie asked.

"I thought I did, I really did. I thought I liked both of them and was falling for both of them, but …" Kara stopped.

Julie could see the look of confusion on Kara's face and asked, "But what?"

"But when I kissed Danger, it just didn't feel like I thought it should," Kara explained with a sigh.

"What did it feel like then?" Julie was so into what Kara was telling her, she was hanging on her every word, "Were his lips too soft or too hard and dry because he's a dirt bike rider or something?"

"Jules! That's not what I meant!" Kara said with embarrassment.

"I know, but were his lips soft? Did it feel good?" Julie asked again.

They were both giggling.

"Oh Julie, it felt so good to kiss him. I am glad he was my first kiss. He has been my friend for so long and so I'm glad we did, but I just didn't feel like it was romantic." Kara was pretending to swoon as she talked, but then stopped as she continued, "I didn't feel the tingling and excitement I thought I would feel inside. It was almost too familiar, you know, like I was kissing a friend, not a boyfriend."

"It's all so clear now," Julie said teasingly, "so what are you going to do?"

"I like them both, I do," Kara said, "but with Danger, it's like we are just good friends and I don't see us being anything but best friends right now."

Julie raised her eyebrow and scrunched her nose, "How rude. I'm right here!"

Kara lightly pushed Julie in a playful way, "I mean, you know that you are my best friend, but Danger is my best guy friend."

"I know, silly, I was just messing with you," Julie said as she pushed Kara in return.

Kara smiled, "After Danger and I talked a while, I think we understand each other on the friend thing. I'm not sure he likes it though …"

Julie interrupted, "No doubt there, he totally loves you. Poor Danger boy." Julie sighed.

Kara sighed again, "Oh no, I don't know if he does or not for sure, but I think he understands where I'm at and that we can still be friends."

"And what about Cru?" Julie asked.

Kara smiled and responded, "I am having so much fun getting to know him and his family. They are so cool and love the water just as much as I do. Did you know that his Dad is a Coast Guard Captain and holds most of the records for swim performance and rescue missions?"

"That's cool!" Julie said.

"I know, right?" Kara confirmed, "They are just like me and love the same things as me. I just have to see where our relationship can go and what develops."

Kara paused and looked down as if she was hiding something.

"Uh, Kara, what aren't you telling me?" Julie inquired, "I can tell when there is something you're not telling me."

Kara hesitated before saying, "Cru tried to kiss me last week, and I didn't let him."

"Ahhhh! Are you serious? Why didn't you tell me?" Julie said, pretending to be mad.

"I just did. I literally just told you," Kara said as she reached over and nudged Julie in a playful manner.

"Funny girl you are not," Julie smirked, "why didn't you let him?"

Kara shrugged and said, "I don't know for sure. I think it is because I have always pictured kissing Danger for my first kiss and I felt like I had to give it a chance with him before just writing off that part of my life's plan." Kara laughed a little giggle, "he he."

"I get it," Julie said assuringly, "That makes sense and now you know."

"Yep; now I know," Kara smiled, "and I think it is going to be fun. No, I know it is going to be fun. It is going to be a great rest of the school year, I can feel it!"

Kara's cell phone buzzed, alerting her to an incoming text message. She looked at her phone.

"Who is it?" Asked Julie.

Kara continued looking at her phone, reading the text, and said with a smile, "Speaking of Cru... It's him, he wants to meet me after practice today."

Then, as if scripted, they both said at the same time, "Let the fun begin."

Kara and Julie laughed and embraced each other in a hug, rocking back-and-forth side-to-side.

Chapter 33 - The Sunset

"What are you going to do after school today?" Asked Greg as Kara prepared for the last day of school.

Kara gave him a funny look and said, "You can hardly call it school today, Dad. All we are going to do the whole day is sign yearbooks."

Greg laughed, "I figured that, but it's still technically school. I'm not so old that I don't remember the last day of high school. Some things never change. What are you doing after all that yearbook fun? I just want to know what time to expect you home tonight, that's all."

"I know," Kara replied, "After we get bored of school yearbook signing, we have plans to meet a group of friends at Tony's diner and do some more signing, you know, make sure we didn't miss any of our friends in the chaos at school. Then Cru and I are going to hang out with some other friends down at the beach, probably for the rest of the night."

Trying to sound as cool as he could, Greg said, "Sounds fun, have a good time and be safe."

"I will, dad, thanks," Kara said.

"Oh, and what about your curfew? Is midnight, as usual, okay or do you think you should get a little more time since it's the last day of school?" Greg said with a grin.

"Oh Dad, really? Can I?" Kara said gleefully.

Greg winked and said, "Sure, honey, as long as you are with your big group of friends, you can stay out a little later, say about 1 o'clock, but if everyone else heads home earlier, please don't just stay out alone with just you and Cru."

Kara responded, "I won't, Dad, I love you! Thanks for the biscuits and gravy, they were delicious!"

"Love you too, sweetheart, have a great day!" Greg said as he gave her a little goodbye hug.

Later that evening, at the beach party, Cru and Kara were sitting down on the sand in the area between the water and some rocks, watching the sunset.

"What are you thinking about?" Cru asked her.

"My mom," Kara said softly.

"Do you think about her often?" he asked kindly.

"A lot, yes, but especially on nights like tonight," she said.

"What is different about tonight?" Cru inquired.

"It's the sunset," Kara said without looking at him, her eyes focused on the horizon, "Watch the sunset as close as you can. Sometimes, right when it is reaching the horizon over the ocean, you can see a green light come up from the water."

"A green light?" he asked.

"Ya," Kara explained, "it's more like a flare, or a flash, or something like that. Kind of like when you can see the vapors from the oil and gas on the road coming up on a hot day."

"Oh, it sounds cool," Cru said with intent interest, "I will watch for it. What else can you tell me about it?"

Kara waited a few moments before saying, "I remember seeing that green flash for the first time when I was very young. I remember feeling like I could hear my mother talking to me when I saw it." She was speaking very slowly, softly, and intently, with her eyes focused on the horizon.

"What would she say to you?" Cru asked, as he moved his hand from her thigh to around her shoulders.

"Just that she loves me and wants me to be happy," Kara said matter-of-factly.

Cru kissed her on the shoulder, "That is so cool! I'm sure she does."

"You don't think it is silly sounding?" Kara said as the inflection in her voice raised slightly.

"No way, I think it is awesome!" Cru assured her, "You have never talked much about your mom, but I can tell you love her very much, even though she has never been with you…in person, I mean."

"Cru?" Kara leaned into his arms and chest.

"What is it?" he asked softly.

"That is one of the reasons I love swimming so much," she said.

"Why?" Cru asked.

Kara paused and sighed quietly before she said, "Whenever I am in the water, I feel like my Mom is with me. I feel like she is hugging me and loving me. There are times when I just can't get enough and I spend several hours, even the whole day in the water."

"Wow," Cru said happily, "that is so cool Kara!"

"Do you really think so?" Kara asked him.

"Hell yes I do!" Cru said a little louder, "I mean, it is sad that you don't have your Mom with you, but it is so cool that you have something that helps you cope with that loss. Something special and unique that helps you feel close to her." Cru kissed her on the forehead.

"My Dad always told me that I was born of the sea," Kara said, "I feel like that is why I always relate swimming with my Mom and why I love it so much?"

"That makes perfect sense why you feel the way you do about being in the water," Cru said compassionately.

The sun had reached the bottom of the horizon and then disappeared below the distant sea. Neither of them saw a green flash. It didn't happen on this particular night.

"Sorry there wasn't a green light for you to see," Kara said. "I really wanted to show it to you."

"No worries, I loved hearing you describe it and the way it makes you feel. We will look for it another time, I'm sure." Cru gave her another kiss on the forehead.

"It's a date then?" Kara said as she nudged him with her elbow, "It is usually easier to see when you are out away from the shoreline farther. I almost always see it when I'm on my Dad's boat."

"It's definitely a date!" Cru said confidently, "Let's do it."

"What do you mean?" Kara playfully asked.

"I mean, let's go out tomorrow night at sunset," Cru suggested. "We can take one of my Dad's boats and we can watch for the green flash."

Kara smiled and said, "Okay, that sounds fun!"

"Plus," Cru added, "there is something else I want to show you as well."

"Something else what?" Kara inquired.

"You will just have to wait to see tomorrow," he said as he squeezed Kara gently with his arms.

"Oh, just tell me," she insisted nicely, "you and your surprises all the time…"

Cru rocked them back and forth as he said, "I'm sorry, but I can't. I have to show you. It can't be explained without being shown in person. You'd never believe me."

"How rude," Kara said jokingly, "of course I'd believe you silly!"

"Kara babe," Cru said, "believe me, then, when I tell you that I have to show you in person."

"That's fair," Kara said as she kissed Cru gently on his neck and quietly said, "it's a date then."

Chapter 34 - He Saved My Life

"Dad?" Kara said to Greg, while they were out for breakfast the next day at one of the local cafés.

"What honey?" he responded.

"Cru wants to take me out on one of his Dad's boats tonight," Kara began her question, "Is that okay?"

"I don't know honey," he said after a little hesitation, "I wish we would have been able to get together with them sometime so I could've met his parents. I'm sorry things have been so busy for me the last few months."

"It's okay, Dad, they were busy too," Kara said kindly.

Greg asked her, "Can you tell me a little bit more about them?"

"Well," Kara thought for a minute, but didn't know exactly what to tell her father, "they are a Coast Guard family."

Greg seemed surprised and said, "What? Really? Why haven't you ever told me that?"

Kara wondered why it was a big deal, but said, "I meant to; I guess it just never came up. Sorry, sorry dad."

"No worries," he said, "I guess things have come up for me too and we haven't talked all that much about them. I don't even know their last name."

"Requin," Kara said as she took a bite of food.

"As in Captain Requin?" Greg sounded very surprised.

"That's the one," Kara said nonchalantly.

"Cru's Dad is Captain Requin, and you never told me?" Greg asked, as if he was a little disappointed.

"I'm sorry, Dad," Kara said sincerely, "I didn't realize it was such a big deal to know exactly who his Dad was. Why?"

"Well," Greg paused, his eyes beginning to water, "Captain Requin... he saved my life."

"Are you serious right now?" Kara put both her hands down on the table with a light slapping noise.

Greg, still teary eyed, said, "Very serious. It was a long time ago, when I was out with Grandpa and his fishing crew. I was just a teenager when one of the worst storms any of us had ever seen hit us."

"You told me about that storm, I think," Kara stated.

"I believe I have, it was the second worst storm I have ever been in," Greg said, "but I haven't told you everything. Something happened that night that I just couldn't explain."

"Like what?" Kara asked, very intrigued by what her Dad was saying.

Greg took a sip of his drink, pushed it up to the top of his plate and leaned forward, saying, "Grandpa had already put in a distress call to the Coast Guard when the storm knocked the steering out of the boat and knocked me in the water at the same time. I was under the water for a long time, or at least that's what I was told. The first thing I remember seeing when I came to my senses, still under water, was the deep depths of the ocean moving farther away from me. I was being pulled to the surface, seemingly faster than I thought possible. I turned to look at the rescue line I assumed was attached to me, but there was not one. I was being pulled by the strongest swimmer I have ever seen. The speed at which he was getting us to the surface seemed super-human!"

"Wow," Kara had put her silverware down and was hanging on every word Greg said.

"That's not even the most amazing part... As we approached the surface at a very quick rate, he gave me a jerk and literally tossed me, with only his right arm, into the arms of your Grandpa and one of his crew, who were leaning out to help. It was amazing," Greg had a dumfounded look on his face, "simply amazing." Greg rocked back in his chair, then leaned forward again, "The strength that that man had was unmatched, unreal even," and then he said slowly, "that man, who saved my life that day, was who you now know as Captain Requin, Cru's Dad."

"Dad, that's amazing! I can't believe it," Kara was crying when her phone alerted her to a text from Cru. She looked at her phone quickly, then looked back at her Dad.

"It's okay, honey," Greg said, "you can read and answer that."

The text said, "Can I pick you up at 7?"

Even though he said it was okay, Kara didn't want to interrupt or make light of what her Dad just told her, so she politely told him she was just going to respond to Cru quickly.

"No thx, I want to come to your house. Will your dad be home?" Kara texted back to Cru.

"I think so, unless he gets called out, why?" Cru asked, "Is everything okay?"

"Yeah," Kara wrote, "I just need to tell him something."

"Um, okay. That's kind of weird. Should I be nervous?" Cru texted with a confused look emoji.

"No, don't worry," Kara said, "I will see you at seven."

Greg reached over and put his hand on Kara's, "I trust the Requin family. Of course you can go out on the boat with Cru tonight."

"Thank you, Dad," Kara said, "I love you. Thank you for telling me more details about your rescue. It means a lot to me."

"I know sweet girl," Greg said, "I love you too; have fun tonight. I will wait up for you."

After they finished breakfast, Greg dropped Kara off at the practice track. Danger was already on his bike, taking some warm-up laps. Kara got her gear on and joined him. As soon as she rode up along the side of him, he gassed the bike, and took off like he was in a race.

"It's gonna be like that, huh?" Kara thought to herself as she sped up to race along with him.

When they had made a couple of laps at full speed, they came to a stop and took off their helmets to talk.

"Nice move," said Danger.

"So what's up with a spontaneous race?" Kara asked.

Danger laughed and said, "I just wanted to see if you were still on top of your game."

"Why wouldn't I be?" Kara said sarcastically.

"Oh, you know, all the time you spend with that swimmer boy," Danger said, "while I am out here practicing without you."

"Knock it off Danger," Kara said, "I thought you said you weren't going to do the jealousy thing."

Danger replied in a defensive tone, "Nah, I'm not jealous. I just want to make sure my teammate is riding to the best of her ability."

Kara could sense the sarcasm and matched it right back, "Gee, thanks, you're the best training partner in the history of the world, Danger boy."

"Funny; very funny," Danger lifted his leg like he was about to start his bike, and yelled enthusiastically, "Let's hit the jumps now lover girl!"

Chapter 35 - Out for a Swim

Kara was standing at the underground front door of the Requin home waiting for someone to answer. She had been given access and permission to just come in anytime she wanted, but did not feel like doing so on today's visit.

As Cru's Dad opened the door, Kara lunged toward him, threw her arms around him, giving him a big hug.

Captain Requin returned the embrace, and said softly, "He told you, didn't he?"

"Yes he did," Kara said, now crying, and speaking softly, but also clearly, "Thank you so much; thank you so, so much for saving my Dad's life! I would not exist if it weren't for you!"

They hugged for a few more moments and then Kara released, stepped back, and said, "Wait a minute, you knew this whole time who my father was, and you never said anything?"

"I'm sorry, Kara, I thought it would be better if it came from him," Captain Requin responded.

"Yes, you are right," Kara paused, "but how did you know he was my Dad, how did you remember him? It was so long ago."

Captain Requin got a reflective look on his face and said, "I remember all my saves. They become part of my life, almost like they are my family. Some of them I might stay in touch with, some of them I don't, but I remember them all."

Cru and his Mom walked in as Kara said, "That is so cool, thank you again," and she gave him another hug.

"What's going on in here?" Asked Cru.

Kara looked at Cru and said, as she held his Dad's arm at the elbow, "I just found out today that your Dad saved my Dad's life when he was a teenager."

"What, really? That is so cool," Cru responded with a smile, walking over to give Kara a welcome hug, "that is so, so cool!" he repeated.

"Do you kids want to have something to eat before you head out?" Asked Cru's Mom.

"Thanks, but we don't have time. We need to get out away from the shoreline before sunset," Cru answered.

"Are you sure?" she asked.

"Yes, Mom," Cru said to her, "I packed some stuff for us."

Kara leaned into Cru and said, "Do they know why we are going out?"

Crus' parents looked at each other and partially smiled like they were surprised. Cru spoke up, "Ya, I told them about wanting to watch the sunset," then he whispered in Kara's ear, "I didn't tell them everything."

"Are you taking the Bay Cruiser?" Cru's Dad asked.

"I was planning on it," Cru answered, "is that okay?"

"Sure," his Dad said, "that old thing oughta get you out far enough from shore in time for the sunset."

"Thanks Dad," Cru turned to Kara, took her hand and said, "You ready?"

The two of them headed upstairs to the family dock and headed out to sea. It was a beautiful evening on the bay as they headed out to the Gulf.

"I feel very good about tonight," Kara said to Cru as the cool evening air swirled around them.

Cru smiled and said, "So do I."

Kara continued, "I feel at peace tonight, like I usually do when I'm thinking of my Mom and especially on nights when I am able to see the green flash. I think it will be a good night."

"I sure hope so," Cru said as he gently rubbed Kara's upper back with his free hand, the other holding the steering wheel.

"What do you mean, 'sure hope so?' Could something be wrong?" Kara asked.

Cru answered, "Oh, I mean I hope we are able to see what you want to show me and I hope you're able to see what I want to show you."

"Oh ya, the surprise. Should I be worried?" Kara said with a playful tone.

"Trust me," Cru said, "it's going to be fine."

The boat they were in was very fast and it was only a few minutes before Kara said, "I think we are out far enough."

Cru responded, saying, "Is it okay if we go just a little farther? We are making good time."

"Sure," Kara said, "just a few more minutes though, we need the boat and water around us to be nice and calm when the sun sets."

Shortly after that, Cru guided the boat to a stop, and it became motionless, with the exception of some mild movement of the tide, up and down. The sea was very calm that evening.

"This is perfect," Kara said, "now look out to the west, the sun is almost to the horizon."

Cru put his feet up on the back of the boat as they sat next to each other, his arm around Kara, holding her close to him.

"So beautiful," he whispered.

"It is, isn't it?" Kara said.

"Yes," Cru said, "and the sunset is too."

Kara looked at Cru who was staring directly in her eyes, something she truly loved about him, but she wanted him to focus on the sunset tonight.

"That's sweet, thank you, but please take this seriously, Cru," said Kara.

"I am," He said, "I just want you to know how I feel about you. I think you are God's most beautiful creation and I consider myself the luckiest man alive every time I am with you."

Kara gave him a kiss on the cheek, "Thank you; now please watch the sun. It's very important to me."

Cru turned to look at the sunset, just as it was reaching the horizon, and the green lights began to show between the sea and the sun. They started very small, and grew to a larger light, or flash, that literally looked like the image of a person standing on the sun.

"Whoa," he said loudly, but calm, "that is amazing! How have I never seen this before?"

Kara said nothing.

Cru looked at her and saw that she was crying. He put his other arm around her and held her tight for a few moments. She then stood up and leaned on the edge of the boat, reaching her arms out in front of her, and then brought them back to her chest, like she was giving herself a hug. Cru just watched her. There was a noticeable peace about her; a noticeable peace about the situation and atmosphere. And then it was gone…the green light was gone. The sun continued on its path and dropped below the horizon.

"Are you okay?" Cru inquired sincerely.

Kara was in tears, "Yes, I am fine."

Cru asked her, "Why the tears?"

"I could hear her tonight," Kara answered.

"You could hear your Mom?" Cru asked, "Really?"

"Yes, I did," Kara said, "remember I told you sometimes I felt she was speaking to me and especially when I see the green flash."

Cru briefly paused before responding, "Yes, I remember. What did she say?"

"I felt like she just said everything is going to be alright," Kara said, "but I don't know what she means. I thought everything was alright already. It kind of scares me, like maybe something bad is going to happen."

"Don't be scared, Kara," Cru was trying to reassure her that they were okay.

"Of what?" Kara asked, "I didn't say I was scared."

Cru paused again, looked at the water, then back at Kara, "There are only a few more minutes of light and I still need to show you something." He began taking off his clothes.

"Cru, what are you doing?" Kara asked innocently.

"I need to get in the water," He said quickly, "What I need to show you requires me in the water."

Kara was curious. As much as she loves the water, she was curious to see what it had to do with what Cru wanted to show her. She simply said, "Okay, I guess, should I join you?" She then answered her own question, "Oh shoot, I can't, I did not bring my suit. I didn't think we were swimming tonight."

"Just me tonight, babe," then Cru dove in the water headfirst and did not resurface for several seconds. Kara was just watching, just as she had been told. When he resurfaced, he only came out of the water up to his eyes.

"Just watch, Kara, and do not be afraid," it was Cru's voice Kara was hearing, but his mouth was still under the water.

"How did you do that?" Kara asked, "I literally just heard you talking to me, but your mouth is under the water."

"Look at my eyes," Kara heard him talking again, but could only see his eyes and not his mouth, but she did what he told her and looked deep into his eyes. He was looking at her deeper than she had ever felt before, she closed her eyes slowly, then opened them again, and thought, instinctively, without speaking, "Okay Cru, show me what you want to show me."

"I think you are ready," Cru had heard her and responded to her in the same thoughtful way, he knew they had a connection of their minds.

Then he sank quickly, as if he was pulled under by an unseen force.

This scared Kara and she yelled into the water, "Cru?" Hoping he was okay, she yelled again, "Cru? Where are you?"

Kara could not see him for what seemed like several minutes gone by, "Cru!" She yelled again and again as she walked to the other side of the boat, "Cru, are you hiding from me? Knock it off right now!"

Then, as she was looking into the water, desperately trying to find Cru, she saw a dorsal fin come around the front of the boat. She screamed with terror.

"Cru! Get out of the water Cru! There is a shark!," She yelled as loud as she could, "Get out of the water now!!"

She felt so helpless yelling into the increasingly dark waters. Then she heard Cru's voice clearly say, "It's okay Kara, I am right here."

Kara turned around abruptly, expecting to see him behind her, but he was not.

"Kara," she heard him say again, "remember not to be scared, everything is going to be okay. I am right here. I got you."

"Where? Where are you, Cru?" She said into the night air.

She then heard him say to her, "Go to the edge of the boat and do not be afraid. Do not move, what you see *will not* hurt you. I promise."

Kara hesitated, but felt a strange peace in the terrifying situation, a peace and calm that was a result of hearing Crus' voice. She managed to go to the edge of the boat and lean out over the water. The dorsal fin was approaching very slowly.

"Do not be afraid," she heard Cru say again, "He will not hurt you. I will not hurt you."

Kara was so confused, but just as she heard those words from Cru, the shark surfaced enough so Kara could see his eyes. They looked just like Cru. The mighty sea creature stopped right in front of her, just looking at her, almost like it was staring at her.

Kara was trying her best to be brave, which she felt surprisingly calm about. She was terrified, but felt at peace at the same time, something which was not common for her. She looked into the shark's eyes and instinctively said, "Cru? Is that you?"

As soon as the words left her mouth, she could not believe she had said it, "Did I really?"

Kara could not believe what was happening. She curled her arms up and just started thinking to herself that she must be having an awful dream. She closed her eyes, then opened them, "Did I just talk to a shark?" She thought to herself as she backed away and sat down.

"Yes, you did," Cru said, "but don't be afraid. It is me. This is me."

Kara closed her eyes again, then opened them. "This has to be a dream," she insisted to herself, "this has to be a dream. This is not really happening."

"This is real Kara," she heard Cru say, "This is what I needed you to know about me. This is what I needed you to know about my family. It's who we are. You do not have anything to fear, though, I am the same boy, you have known for almost a year now. I am Cru."

"Cru!?" She yelled, "Cru!?" She was crying hysterically now, "Cru, where are you?"

"I am here," she heard, as the shark rose up on the side of the boat.

This scared her even more and Kara screamed again, "Cru, if that is really you, you get in this boat and take me home right now."

The shark sank back into the ocean for a few seconds and then Cru, as a man, jumped up out of the water like a fish, and approached Kara, "It's okay, Kara, it's me. It's only me."

Kara did not look at him. She just turned away and said to him, "Take me home please."

Chapter 36 - It's not me you need to talk to

Cru was driving his Dad's boat as fast as he could toward the coastline. He was trying to get Kara to talk to him, but she would not.

He was pleading with her, "Kara, it's okay with me that you are in shock or whatever. I knew there was no way I could reasonably expect you to understand this. But please know that the way I feel about you has not changed and I hope the way you feel about me has not changed. I just needed you to know who and what I am."

Kara did not respond. Seeing that she was now within cell phone distance to make a call, she reached into her jacket to get her phone and dialed her Grandma.

"Grammy?" She said, crying.

"Kara, is that you?" Her Grandma asked, "Where are you, honey, and what is the matter?"

Kara answered, "Grammy, I need to talk to you, are you home?"

"Yes, darling, we are home. Where are you?" Helen asked.

Kara said, "I am in the bay with Cru, headed to shore; I will be there in a few minutes."

Kara then turned to Cru and said, "Please drop me off at my grandparents dock."

As soon as Cru reached the dock, he said, "Kara, I know what happened tonight is hard to understand, but it is real. It is me. Please call me when you're ready to talk to me about it."

Kara was looking into his eyes as he spoke to her and then got out of the boat and ran inside her grandparents house.

Helen had been watching for her and met her at the door with a warm embrace, "Kara, sweetie, is everything okay?"

Kara was still sobbing, "I don't know Grammy. I just don't know."

"Did he hurt you?" Helen asked, as Robert came to them.

"No, he didn't hurt me," Kara said.

They hugged until Kara was a little more calm and Helen said, "Why don't we go sit down in the kitchen and talk? I will have your Grandpa go get us some ice cream."

"Thanks Grammy," Kara said, "but I don't think I can eat ice cream right now."

"Oh, my dear Kara, what happened tonight? Did Cru break up with you?" she asked.

Kara responded quickly, but softly, "No, he didn't."

Helen followed with, "Did you break up with him?"

"No," Kara said.

Grandma waited a moment, and then said "What then, darling? I am happy to help, but you need to tell me something so I can start to understand."

Kara just continued crying and Helen moved over to her again and held her, letting her cry on her shoulder. Then, after a few more moments, she said, "I'm sorry I was pushing you, you just get the tears out first. Take your time and we will talk when you are ready."

"Grammy?" Kara spoke very softly, almost whispering, and whimpering at the same time.

"I am here for you," her Grammy said, "what is it sweetheart?"

"Am I awake?" Kara was still feeling like this might just be a dream.

Helen, confused by the question, still answered normally, saying, "Yes, you are awake."

"Then I don't know what is real anymore," Kara said.

"What do you mean, Kara? Is it Cru?" Helen asked, "Boys can be very hard to understand sometimes."

"Yes," Kara said, "it's Cru, but it's not like that. It is so much more than just a hard to understand teenage boy."

"What is it? Please tell me," Helen put her hand on Kara's head and pulled it under her chin.

"Tonight Cru turned into a shark," Kara said clearly.

There was silence. Dead silence. Even the bugs outside and the sounds of the water seemed to stop. It was totally silent and totally still.

Helen broke the silence to her granddaughter by saying very slowly, "Did you just say that Cru turned into a shark?"

"I know, Grammy," Kara said as she sat up tall and let go of her Grandma, "I know it is hard to believe, but I saw it with my own eyes. He turned into a shark, talked to me with his mind, then turned back into Cru."

There was more silence as Helen stood up and walked to her cupboard, obviously in deep thought.

"You think I am crazy or something, don't you Grammy?" Kara asked meekly.

There was no response.

"Grammy, are you sure I am not dreaming? Because if I am dreaming, I just want to wake up," Kara began pinching herself, and slapping herself in the face.

"Stop, Kara, you are not dreaming," Helen turned around, with tears streaming down her face, looking directly at Kara, totally peaceful, and said, "It is not me you need to talk to."

"What do you mean Grammy?" she asked.

"You need to go talk to your father about this," Helen said as lovingly as she possibly could.

"But Grammy," Kara pleaded, "I always talk to you about boy troubles. My dad won't understand."

"Kara, this is not a boy problem," Helen said, "This is more; and I promise you, with all the tenderness in my heart and in his, that your Dad will understand."

Helen walked over to Kara and gave her another big hug, "Go talk to your father; he will understand what happened to you tonight."

Kara paused and looked at her Grandma for a few moments, "Thank you, Grammy, I feel better, even though I have no idea what you were talking about or what happened tonight."

"Just tell your father what you saw tonight," Helen said to Kara.

Robert drove Kara home and Helen texted her son on the way, "You need to tell Kara everything tonight. She is on her way home, Bob is driving her."

As Kara walked into her home, Greg was waiting for her in the living room, just like he usually is when he is home and she has been out.

"Hi honey, how was your night?" pretending that he didn't know.

"Do you know or are you really asking me?" Kara said, sensing her dad did not sound at ease.

"Well," he said, "your grandma texted me and told me I needed to talk to you, but that's all."

"Dad, I am so confused," Kara said, crying again, as she sat next to him and put he head on his arm.

"About what?" Grag asked.

"About what I saw tonight," Kara then sat back up and told her father everything that had happened to her that evening, describing everything in detail, including seeing the green flash, and feeling like her mother had spoken words of peace to her.

"Dad, what happened tonight, I don't understand?" Kara pleaded, "If you know something, please just tell me. Am I dreaming? I just want this to be over."

"Kara, my sweet daughter, you are not dreaming. What you heard and saw tonight was very real," Greg got up from the couch and slowly walked to the fireplace, then over to the window and slid it open; his back towards Kara as he looked deeply in the direction of the sea. He stood there for a few moments, then blew a kiss into the night air and made a gesture of catching one back, then holding it to his heart with his hand.

"Dad, please tell me what you are talking about," Kara was being so nice about it as she spoke in a pleading tone.

Greg was quiet, he did not say a word, just took a deep breath as he turned to face his daughter.

"Dad, please tell me what you know. I can feel it now. I think I am ready, I feel like there is so much more for you to tell me than just what I saw tonight." Kara was no longer crying and spoke very clearly and confidently.

"I think you are ready too, Kara," Greg responded in the same tone.

"Okay, what do you have to say then?" Kara asked, one last time.

Greg began, "Kara, there is something I need to tell you about your Mom…"

Made in United States
Troutdale, OR
11/02/2024